Other titles available in the Savannah Stories Series

Payback

First Comes Love

Tainted Love

With This Ring

Angel Unaware

Blood Lust

Revelations

Cooking Up Trouble

Other titles from J.L. Lemon

Second Chances

The Savannah Stories

Blast From The Past

The Savannah Stories

Blast From The Past

J.L. Lemon

ISBN-13: 978-0-9909589-1-8

Published 2007
Second Edition 2015

Printed by Lulu.com in the United States of America

For my parents who have always been a bountiful fountain of

encouragement and support.

Advise no one to go to war or marry

- Spanish proverb

Prologue

A New Partner

Her Story

She first met Ennis Rutherford when they were assigned as partners. Her captain, Josh Hunter, knocked on her office door while she typed a report on the computer, "Your new partner's here. Ennis, Savannah Prince. Savannah, Ennis Rutherford."

She didn't look up from her work but kept on typing, "Dennis, huh?"

"Ennis, actually. No D," a deep baritone voice corrected. That voice halted her work instantly. She had pictured a man about her height who resembled more of a scrawny rookie, too scared to piss off the higher ups. From what Josh told her, Ennis was from Texas, the gunslinger capital of the nation. When she lifted her vision to her new partner, he all but stole her breath. He wore a dark blue suit with light blue dress shirt and no tie. There wasn't a scrawny ounce on the man – he stood a strapping six foot two, broad shouldered and burly, his body built like a football player. The shadow of stubble enhanced his handsome face along with his dark wavy hair cut above his collar, and his coffee brown eyes seemed to warm the instant their eyes met. She wasn't sure if it was a curse or joke to be blessed with this slice of heaven before her. Someone had a wicked sense of humor for presenting her with this obvious temptation. If they grew 'em this handsome in Texas, maybe there was something to the cowboy mystique after all, she decided.

She shook her head, ridding herself of the fanciful romantic ideas and outright forbidden fantasies. She reclaimed her professional frame of mind, offered an apology to her partner, "Ennis is just an unusual name around these parts."

His lips curved into an easy, charming smile. Her cheeks warmed until Josh Hunter's eyes widened. Now she felt embarrassed by the blush. Oh God, Hunter knows, she thought. He knows I'm attracted to Ennis Not Dennis.

Judging by Ennis Not Dennis's expression, he also sensed it. "Well, the name Savannah's not typical in Texas so we're even." He thrust his hand out and she rose from the computer and rounded the desk.

When his hand wrapped around hers, it felt strong and warm. His thumb seemed to caress the back of her hand, not in a brazen way but a friendly one. The simple motion sent a tingle up her arm, "Ennis Rutherford. I guess everything *is* bigger in Texas, even surnames." And detectives, she added, noticing how his eyes complimented his smile. Rich, warm brown eyes that invited a woman to step into his arms and plant one hell of a lingering kiss those smiling lips. "Boss said you transferred from the Amarillo Police Department." He also said Ennis was promoted to detective shortly before leaving Amarillo. Mr. Rutherford climbed the ladder fast, she noted, since he was three years her junior. She'd been a detective four years and she fast approached thirty. "Exactly where is Amarillo?" Lord, she really dreaded letting go of his hand.

He didn't seem too anxious to release her hand either, "It's in the Panhandle."

The Panhandle explains everything - not. She never professed to being a genius however she was used to the Florida Panhandle and the Nebraska and Oklahoma Panhandles 'cause they looked like actual pan handles. Was he telling her that square thumb sticking straight up out of Texas was a Panhandle?

Seeing her quandary, he explained, "It's beneath the Oklahoma Panhandle. I grew up in Vega, a little town about forty miles west of Amarillo."

Yep. Ennis Not Dennis came from the Square Thumb of

Texas, or Panhandle as he called it. "And how big is Amarillo?"

"About a hundred seventy thousand people or so."

"Much crime there?"

"Enough, why?"

"'Cause you just moved to one of the highest crime areas of the nation, especially in summertime," she capped off the statement with a sneeze. She turned to her desk to find a tissue, "We're also the allergy capital."

Ennis's hand went straight to his hip pocket and withdrew a handkerchief which he presented to her.

Incredulous, her brow lifted. He offered her his handkerchief? Did men do that anymore? Hell, did men still *carry* those things? She supposed so, if they were from the Square Thumb.

"Go ahead," he assured, nudging it at her. "It's clean, I promise."

Savannah took the handkerchief from him and wiped her nose with a word of thanks. "You always this chivalrous?"

"I try to be, yes. Especially with beautiful women." He quickly backtracked, "No offense by that."

"None taken." How could she possibly take offense? With that voice and that tender smile he laid on her, she'd be silly to take offense... *Wait*, she thought. *Did I just use the word "tender" to describe my new partner? Oh, for God's sake...*

O O O

"It's not gonna work," she told her sister Georgia that night at dinner. She stewed all day over it – well, when she wasn't busy daydreaming about Ennis Rutherford, that was. Savannah gripped her fork harder, debating over whether to jab herself good and hard so she'd stop thinking about him.

"What's not?"

"This new partner. His name's Ennis Rutherford. Not Dennis but Ennis." She speared her fork into the thick Omaha steak and began slicing off a piece with a little too much vehemence.

Her sister just stared at the utensils moving vigorously through the meat, "What's wrong with him?"

"He's too damn nice."

Georgia laughed, "*That's* why it won't work?" She began cutting her own steak, but at a reasonable pace, "How many years have you prayed for a decent partner?"

"You don't understand, Georgia. He's nice. Like genteel nice, like Ashley Wilkes nice, like *he won't last* nice." She hacked at the steak, "And so good looking," she finally sighed, giving her fork and knife a breather. "He's right out of a men's underwear catalog. I can't work around someone like that. Talk about a Biblical temptation…"

Georgia's green eyes sparkled, "And you get to work with him every day."

Foregoing a smile, Savannah replied, "You're not exactly helping." She didn't appreciate the trivial attitude Georgia chose to place on her current situation. This was serious. Savannah wasn't paired with a "Hunk of the Month" she was paired with a "Hunk of a Lifetime". No assembly required, all parts present and accounted for, even the friendly personality, generosity and perfect manners. "He won't last because he's too good to be true and then I'll get yet another partner. I'll be the only cop that their partners outnumber their years on the job."

Georgia shrugged, "If he doesn't last, at least you can act on those Biblical temptations you mentioned. Till then, enjoy the view."

His Story

He'd met Savannah Prince on a Tuesday. Fall was in its infancy with cooler mornings that thankfully diminished the stifling humidity. Ennis never felt so sticky in his life since moving to

Atlanta.

Knowing only a few things about his new partner, he chose a dark blue suit – a neutral color – just in case she was as bitchy as he'd heard. No one hated the color blue, did they? Before allowing his new captain to introduce them, he headed off to the bathroom to regroup his approach. Prince, in her late twenties, was by most accounts moody, hardheaded and maybe even gay since no one ever saw her with a man. No one ever saw her with another woman either so Ennis decided to leave the "gay" notion alone until further investigation. Also, by most accounts, she was undeniably beautiful. He'd walk in and take stock of the situation and pray moving to the South wasn't as bad an idea as his family feared.

Josh Hunter introduced them which, Ennis could tell, didn't impress Detective Prince in the least. She continued pecking away at the computer's keyboard, dismissing his presence with a ho-hum attitude. Then she called him Dennis. From her reputation, he wondered if she'd done it to irritate him. From her posture at the computer, he realized it was indifference. Mentally he ran through what he knew about her past with partners. Most were either criminals or plain do-nothings. From her point of view, Ennis understood why she felt apathetic toward him. She probably thought the higher ups had shoveled another asshole her way.

When she finally decided to notice him, she turned and looked straight at him. What started as a judging glare melted into what he hoped was stunned silence. Well, they were Even Steven on that count. He couldn't find his voice or his right mind upon casting eyes on her. He'd seen this woman before. She vaguely resembled a film star from long ago. His mind, still tripping over itself, at last stumbled on the name. Rita Hayworth. She looked reminiscent of the Love Goddess in her facial features and dark wavy hair. Savannah's was a shining chestnut color unlike Hayworth's flaming red but the effects remained the same. Ennis fell instantly in lust.

In her sultry voice he detected a light southern drawl, not the heavy brogue associated with Scarlett O'Hara but a delicate, more charming inflection.

She rose, stretching into a tall, lanky five foot nine inch dream. His hand wrapped around hers, nearly swallowing it whole. A dark blush crept into her cheeks, dispelling any assumption the woman was gay. Ennis planned to keep that little secret to himself or some other cop would move in on his pretty new partner.

By her handshake, he learned that her figure contradicted her strength. Savannah's trim physique shouted fragile but as he later discovered, she could wrestle successfully with decently built men. Their first arrest proved her effectiveness as a cop. While chasing a rather beefy suspect, Ennis nearly laughed when she grabbed the back of the guy's jacket collar. Ennis didn't laugh when she stopped while jerking the man backwards. The suspect lost his footing and fell back like she'd clotheslined him. With his fight temporarily tamed, Savannah offered a helping hand to the suspect. In his mind, Ennis knew they'd end up chasing him again. The guy was too eager to grab her hand. Ennis shook his head and waited for the guy to overpower her and pull her to the ground. He waited for nothing. The moment the guy's hand closed around hers, she hauled him up, slammed him over the hood of their detective's car, forced his feet wide apart with a couple of solid kicks then cuffed him – without an ounce of assistance from Ennis. No, he certainly didn't want Savannah mad at him. Not when she resembled a rogue Charlie's Angel when angry.

Evidently being labeled "bitchy" hardly ruffled her feathers. Mostly Ennis figured she protected herself from uninvited advances from other cops while trying to watch her back with the higher ups. One thing he could say: Savannah Prince knew how to clam up. It irritated her when he'd ask questions about her or her life. It didn't matter, she'd say to which he'd respond that it mattered to him. Those words prompted a wary glance and a "why" from her.

She was such an enigma to him, Ennis found himself seeking answers from their captain. Josh Hunter became a fountain of information and basically taught him the basic ins and outs of Savannah's personality. She was the youngest of three children, her brother Seth being the oldest, her sister Georgia the middle child. Their mother passed away when Savannah was eighteen but Hunter hadn't furthered the topic past that. Ennis cringed when Hunter divulged Savannah grew up in an abusive home. He told his new detective these things, he said, to avoid any awkward conversations later. Because she was mighty touchy about certain subjects, her father's abuse and her mother's passing in particular. The Prince family owned apple and pecan orchards outside Augusta, Savannah's hometown. As for her abilities on the job, she was a good, solid detective, loyal to the bone and an asset to the department.

Ennis woke up each morning with a goal – to sway his partner into a dinner date with him, or even a drink after shift. From there, he'd let nature take its course. Because one thing he knew. Despite her temper, her quirks regarding certain subjects, and that tenacious little gleam in her blue eyes, this woman was worth investigating from head to toe. If given half a chance, he'd give Savannah Prince something to *really* blush about.

1

"Savannah," a man called from her office doorway.

The voice wasn't readily familiar. "Hold on a sec. I'm nearly done here." She continued typing, completing the formalities of hers and Ennis's last case. Five more entries and she could send the file to their boss.

Her computer faced the wall, her back to the door. She arranged it that way by necessity. The office was tiny with little legroom, both sitting and standing. There was barely enough room for her desk and two chairs, let alone a computer table.

With pencil perched in mouth and fingers steadily pounding the keyboard, relief washing over her as she closed the door on another case.

"Come on, sweetheart," the voice urged lovingly.

Her fingers slowed their movement. Having no real love interest, Savannah wondered who felt secure enough to call her "sweetheart" without fear of losing some teeth. Ennis called her cute names but this wasn't Ennis and the name wasn't said in a casual fashion. The man *meant* it.

"Come here, sweetheart. Come to Daddy," he invited, his voice growing softer with each word.

That did it. In one fluid movement, she spun in her chair and faced the presumptuous male guest. Then, as her jaw dropped, the pencil fell out of her mouth, rolled down her leg and onto the floor. *Close your mouth,* her brain implored. *You look stupid.*

The mental berating had no actual effect on her jaw that continued to defy her. Her stomach suddenly pitched and rolled like a ship on choppy waters. Her right kidney panged at the sight before her, throwing her mind eight years in the past.

She yanked open a desk drawer to search for the Tums she kept for such occasions. Rummaging feverishly, she sighed when she found none. She couldn't bring herself to say the words lingering on her tongue. No, those got a cop reprimanded. So she shook her head in disbelief, "Tobias Jerome Jackson as I live and breathe."

Toby hated being called Jerome. It sounded sissified, he'd said when they were together. She'd used the name on purpose for a dash of revenge, she supposed. Mostly it just felt good to aggravate him.

His reaction surprised her, however, when he chuckled, "Savannah Charlene Prince. How've you been?"

"Peachy until," she referenced her watch, "one minute ago. What cat dragged you in?"

He took one step in the office. She straightened in her chair, her brow diving straight down. Heeding the unspoken warning, he stopped.

One look at Toby Jackson brought memories of the charm bracelet he'd stolen before she broke up with him. Toby used her mother's gift to lure her back to his place. With vivid, painful clarity she recalled the night she dropped by for the bracelet. His fist knocking her senseless with a powerful blow. Toby stripping off her jeans. His naked, muscular body crawling atop her, her blurred vision clearing enough to see his thick arousal. And his words squeezed through clenched teeth – *I'm going to enjoy this.*

She'd fought his iron grasp on her wrists, tried angling for leverage against his weight. Her older brother Seth's self-defense training took over and she managed enough space to place her right foot against his hip and shove. Her left foot slammed into his chest, pushing him back then she launched her right heel into his chin, knocking him off her. She gathered her cherished charm bracelet along with the remnants of her clothes and dignity and left with a vow to kill him if she ever saw him again.

"...to look. Savannah," he called. "You okay? You're not listening."

The itch to reach to her holster and make good on her promise became impossible to ignore. He put more bruises on her during their relationship than her father ever had. Sent her to the hospital once too. She'd wanted revenge for so many years the old desire resurfaced along with the ugly memories. It figured their next meeting occurred in a place that prevented her from ventilating the deviant turd.

"What were you saying?" she asked, not really caring.

His vision suddenly darted under her desk. Savannah glanced down to see two shining eyes staring up at her. The little girl, about four, smiled. *Toby's daughter.* She knew by the devilish slant of the grin, by the dark curling hair and the coffee brown eyes. A small hand reached up, offering the pencil to Savannah. She took it, rewarding the girl with a brief smile and thanks.

Toby finally stepped in the office to call his child, "Sandy." He retrieved a piece of candy from his pocket, "You want a Tootsie Roll?"

The little girl scrambled from under the desk to join her father. Joy lit her eyes when he handed her the candy. He put a hand on her shoulder and shrugged at Savannah, "Sorry 'bout that. She likes women, sometimes a little too much."

"Like her daddy." She sighed, irritated, "Tell me why you're here and get out."

"I need your help."

Savannah nearly burst into laughter. Now *that* was funny. Toby needed her help? Like hell she'd help him do anything short of drawing his last breath. Especially after what he'd done to her physically *and* cheated on her with another woman, a fact she uncovered – literally – one evening after her shift. Toby repaid her intrusion with a right cross to her jaw. *Now* he needed *her* help? Yeah. Right.

She paused, recalling a favorite saying of Georgia's. People reap what they sow, she said. Savannah hoped she was right. No one deserved more reaping than Tobias Jackson. She couldn't help it. A smile crept across her lips.

Frowning at her reaction, Toby tried to mask his resentment, "Look, babe, I'm coming to you because I know you and I trust you to do your job."

Something stopped her from unloading on him. What, she wasn't sure, but assumed it had everything to do with the little girl happily chewing on her Tootsie Roll. The kid didn't hurt her. Toby did. With that thought, she stood up and called Ennis into the room.

Her partner stood a few inches taller than Toby and was

all-around beefier. She remembered how muscular Toby was when they were together. He'd lifted her into his arms as if she were a feather in the breeze. Now he appeared thinner and less buff than years earlier but still able to knock a woman unconscious with one hard punch. After introducing Ennis to Toby, she asked her partner to entertain Sandy while she spoke to Toby. The worried little girl clung to her father until he kissed her. Savannah glanced away, wondering if he treated his daughter the same way he treated her. She saw no outward signs of abuse but Toby, unless provoked into a rage, never left bruises visible to others.

Toby watched Ennis escort Sandy by the hand, her partner's usual baritone voice elevating somewhat to talk sweetly to the girl.

"Nice guy," Toby mentioned. "You an item?"

"Unlike you, I don't indiscriminately chase the opposite sex until they either capitulate to my charms or I can tackle them."

Ignoring her icy remark, he focused on her left hand, "I thought you'd be married by now."

"And I thought you'd be dead. Count us both surprised." She put hands to hips, "What kind of help do you need?"

Toby's gaze slid down her body. Though he didn't make

the move obvious, Savannah felt him undressing her in his mind. His vision skimmed up her legs then stopped at her breasts, "You still got the body, babe. Those breasts were always my weakness."

"Before I slap the hell out of you," she lifted his chin with her hand, "tell me why you're here."

He shoved his hands in his pockets, "I can't find my wife. I think something's happened to her."

Yeah, I bet I know what it was too. "Not my department. I deal with people when they're dead, not missing. Is she dead, Toby?"

His eyes widened, "God, I hope not."

Savannah pointed across the hall, "Then you need Missing Persons. It's down the hall to your left." She turned to go back to her desk. She gasped when he grabbed her arm, spinning her back to him. He used enough force to bring her body solidly against his.

The hardness of his chest crushed her breasts, his hold tightening on her arm. She tensed. In the past, a fist came next, whether to the jaw or gut. If he was particularly pissed off, he hit a kidney.

Toby's dark eyes pierced her blue ones. Those blue eyes narrowed, warned him to let go or the .38 nestled at her hip might see some action.

He loosened his grasp but refused to release her, "Listen, I know I hurt you. I regret that. You're a good woman and didn't deserve what I did but we've both moved on. Now my wife is gone and you're the only one I trust to help me."

"And you're sure she didn't tire of being your punching bag or putting up with your philandering ways?"

His face lowered to hers, their lips only a breath away, "I haven't cheated on her."

"Tobias..." she admonished. "For a happily married man, you gave me an inappropriate compliment about my body and breasts a moment ago. If you expect me to believe *my* breasts were your only weakness, think again."

He swallowed whatever comment poised on his tongue. Instead, he kissed her, his lips firm and insistent.

Savannah pulled away, angry. Before withdrawing her .38 and playing shooting gallery on his vital organs, she put some space between them, *"Do that again and I'll cripple you."*

Toby released a long, slow breath – to calm down, she guessed. She felt his body react to the kiss and glanced down at the evidence. He smiled, readjusting his hard-on through his jeans, "You used to like it."

She kept her voice down, "I was drunk back then, if you recall. And you were too."

"Now don't get all pissed off and call me Jerome again," he teased. "Geez, it was just a kiss."

Yes, one kiss. That's all it took eight years ago at a bar too. She spent enough time with Jack Daniels that night to feel good about the rugged, handsome fella down the way. Felt even better when he sidled up beside her, bought her a couple of more shots of Jack. Then he called her beautiful and kissed her. The world tilted sideways and Savannah's existence started on a one year rocky and most painful road.

Savannah curbed the urge to slap him. He treated their meeting as if they parted company on a pleasant note. For him to march in and take such ridiculous and improper liberties as kissing her, well, she needed help restraining herself from committing grievous bodily harm. "Rutherford!" She summoned her partner with a fortitude Scarlett O'Hara would have admired. She couldn't believe tears actually welled in her eyes. Angry ones that brought back the sheer misery and hurt Toby caused.

Within seconds, Ennis appeared at the door with Sandy on his hip, "What's wrong?"

She turned away to wipe the growing tears, "See if Brooks will take the girl. She likes women. I want you in here while we talk."

Ennis leveled an accusing look at Toby, "What did you do?"

She tried to call off her partner, "Since Mr. Jackson and I share a personal history, I need a set of objective ears. His wife is missing."

"Missing Persons, Room 20, down the hall and to the left." Ennis sat Sandy at Toby's feet, "The detective in charge will help you."

Feeling ganged up on, Toby weighed his options. Then he resolutely deposited himself in the chair across from her desk and lifted Sandy into his lap. He had a hint of defiance in his expression and tone, "I can't change the past, Savannah. Go ahead and sic your partner on me. Hell, how about the whole department like you did back then. None of it will change the fact my wife is missing and I want her back."

"I never sicced anyone on you, Toby. They took it upon themselves to teach you a lesson." Why she felt beholden to defend her friends' actions, she wasn't sure. She did know she was grateful to them. Her partner Riley Murphy and her academy buddies (including her new boyfriend Adam Rafferty) saw the bruise on her jaw and beat Toby within an inch of his life. From that day on Toby assumed she was responsible for that beating.

"Whatever." Toby reached in his hip pocket for his

wallet. He removed a photo of himself with his wife.

"Mama," little Sandy pointed at the photo.

Toby kissed her hair, withdrawing into a brief reflective mood, "Yes, sweetheart, that's Mama." He slapped the photo on Savannah's desk, "Lori Evans Jackson. She works for Peaches Realty as do I. I last saw her four days ago before she left for a realtor's convention in your namesake city. It was at the Westin Savannah Harbor Resort. I last heard from her via phone two days ago. I've called everyone we know and they haven't heard a word from her. I called the hospitals here and in Savannah and nothing. It's like she's dropped off the face of the globe. Now, I need your help and you're gonna give it because you really don't want me camping out in your office."

2

Georgia knew something was on Savannah's mind. Her younger sister arrived after her shift – about seven that night – with a quiet but slight edge to her personality. The tense silence stretched through their dinner hour. Georgia puzzled over the drastic change. She'd seen it only a few times before, usually during a particularly gruesome murder case.

Attempts to drag the problem into the open met with failure and Georgia resigned herself to hush and wash the dishes. While Savannah roosted at the dining table, Georgia soaped up the skillet she'd used to fry the catfish.

While rinsing it, she heard Savannah talking on her cell, "Is this the Westin Savannah Harbor Resort? This is Detective Prince with the Atlanta Police. I'm looking for a patron by the name of Lori Jackson. She checked in four days ago for a realtor's convention... My name is Detective Prince. P-r-i-n-c-e..."

Georgia listened to her sister spell her last name through clenched teeth. For that reaction, someone either gave her lip or she highly disliked her current task. "Yeah, that's right," Savannah continued. "She never registered? How about a Lori Evans?" She drummed her fingers on the folder, waiting. "Nothing there either. Okay, then. Thanks."

Georgia dried her hands on a nearby dishcloth, approached the dining table and sat down, "What's going on? Since when do you work Missing Persons?"

Her sister sighed and dropped her head in her hands, "I don't."

Georgia reached toward the open file, "Mind if I take a look?"

Savannah slammed the file shut, "Yes. Stay out of it."

Georgia jerked her hand back as if to save it from sudden amputation. Her concern transformed to annoyance by Savannah's swift, nasty reaction. In response, Georgia hauled off and spanked Savannah's hip with the damp dish towel, "Don't be rude. It was just a question. You've been acting peculiar all night. Like to tell me why?"

"I'm sorry," was the groaned reply. She rested her chin in one hand, "It's a favor. The guy's wife is missing."

Georgia shrugged, "Is it the governor's wife? I don't understand the secrecy. You've always shared your work with me."

Savannah seemingly debated opening the file. She toyed

with the corner, lifted it a bit then closed it again. She repeated this action a few more times before raising her vision to Georgia's, "Don't get pissed." She then opened the file.

Before dropping her vision to the table, Georgia slanted her sister a wary frown. Why would she get angry? She was doing a favor for a friend, which was okay with... The instant her green eyes focused on the wallet sized photo, she felt her gut tighten and her blood pressure skyrocket. "Tobias Jackson? You're looking for Toby's wife?"

"He asked me to –"

"You're doing him a favor after what he did to you?"

"Oh, I see. You're assuming I volunteered for this job. That I stood there saying, 'Hey, asshole, it's okay you beat me black and blue. Just tell me what I can do for *you* today, Mr. Toby I-Am-A-Total-Jerk Jackson.'" Savannah griped with teeth clenched. One fist slammed on the table, rattling the sturdy oak top and the dinner glasses sitting on it. "You think I don't remember what he did to me? I'm not stupid, Georgia. I remember everything," she finished with heavy emphasis on "everything".

Concern furrowed the eldest sister's features. She reached forward, taking Savannah's trembling hand, "Calm down, honey. I didn't mean to upset you like this."

Savannah shook her head while fighting tears, "I've been

upset all day. He comes into my office with his daughter and insists I find his wife. The poor woman's probably dead and that son of a bitch recruited me to find her body. Sounds like him, doesn't it? I only took the case because of the kid. She deserves answers about what's happened to her mother."

Georgia took a deep breath. She'd spent many nights and days like this. Holding her sister's hand while she cried, nursing emotional wounds along with physical ones. All because of that bastard Toby. Georgia was never so grateful for a breakup in her life. When her sister walked away from him, she'd hoped Savannah could reclaim her life and perhaps stop drinking. She reclaimed her life but it took even longer to leave the bottle behind. Georgia prayed the day's interaction with Toby didn't entice her back to drinking. Abstaining equaled a precarious balancing act on a high wire for Savannah. Stress increased her thirst to visit Jack Daniels. Determination prevented her from doing so – that and guilt. Throw Toby into the mix and all bets were off.

Georgia made a mental note to call Ennis later. She would forewarn him to watch Savannah's mood without telling him precisely why, but would express concern about Toby's temper. That's all Ennis Rutherford needed to know because in her heart, Georgia knew he was sweet on Savannah and would protect her with his life.

She flipped the photo face down, "Toby's an evil creature, Savannah. For the longest, I thought Tobias Jackson was listed as a Biblical plague. Somewhere between the frogs and boils."

3

Georgia heard whimpering next to her then realized the covers were thrown to her feet. She began to turn over when a sharp pain registered in her back. She'd invited Savannah to stay the night and now Georgia wondered how smart sharing the same bed was. Since childhood, nightmares plagued the younger sister and fighting through them physically came with the package. This time, however, the nightmare erupted into hurling fists and kicking feet.

Savannah elbowed her again and after expressing her own protest, Georgia flipped over to awaken her sister but Savannah's fist swung back and whacked her shoulder. She heard several mumbled pleas grow in volume as the fight intensified. Bolting upright, Savannah wept while pleading for someone to stop. Georgia would have bet her inheritance the nightmare revolved around Toby.

Georgia took the opportunity to wrap her arms around her sister's taut, trembling body and bring her into an embrace, "Savannah, wake up. You're with me. You're okay."

As if drawn from a sleepwalking daze, Savannah's struggle collapsed into her sister's arms, the tears flowing. She clung to Georgia as she cried, her sobs uncontrollable. Georgia held tight as she had in the past, rocking her baby sister as she released pent-up emotion and long contained fear. She felt Savannah's arms tighten around her as if letting go meant falling into an abyss. An abyss called Toby Jackson.

Georgia stroked her hair and spoke softly, hoping to calm her crying. If she could pull Savannah back from the terror trapping her only moments earlier... "You're safe. No one's going to hurt you," she assured with a whisper. She couldn't imagine the hell tearing through her sister's subconscious – she only knew it took a lot to reduce Savannah to such an emotional mess.

She held Savannah until her breathing settled into a normal rhythm and her crying ebbed to sniffles. She approached the subject cautiously, "Remember when you were a little girl and had nightmares?"

Savannah nodded, the hold on her older sister still firm and solid. Georgia smoothed her hair and continued the gentle rocking motion, "I said that telling someone is like a magic trick. It stops the nightmare from coming back."

"I remember," replied her quavering voice. She reinforced her embrace as if to shore up her courage. "But this one will never go away."

Georgia pursed her lips. She imagined the nightmare revolved around Toby. Savannah went to bed obsessing over him, talking about him and how she figured he'd murdered his wife. "Is it about Toby?" she asked.

Savannah nodded. In her heart, Georgia suspected the theme of the horrific nightmare. She remembered eight years back when Savannah broke off her relationship with him. He'd done everything in his power to entice her back. Flowers (that went in the trash). Phone calls (that went unanswered). A box of chocolates with a silly note reading *You are my sweetheart. Please come back.* When he exhausted other efforts, Mr. Jackson resorted to extortion. Weeks before the breakup, he'd swiped Savannah's cherished charm bracelet hers and Georgia's mother Charlene gave her on her sixteenth birthday. He used it as leverage to drag Savannah back to his place to pick it up. The memory was almost too painful to recall. Later that night when she arrived at Georgia's house, she had the charm bracelet. Along with it she had a bottle of Jack Daniels and the beginnings of a bruise on her jaw. Her ripped blouse hung askew on her slumped shoulders, her panties and bra stuffed haphazardly in the pocket of her jeans. Savannah refused to talk past saying Toby admitted to stealing the bracelet and used it as bait.

Georgia pleaded with her sister to explain what happened, why her clothes were torn, why she limped when she walked, why her panties and bra hung from her pocket? She knew the answer. Toby tried to rape her – or *had* raped her. But Savannah refused to confess the details of the evening. Instead, with tears streaming down her face, she hugged the bottle of Jack closer then trudged upstairs for a bath.

After Savannah retired for the night, Georgia tidied up the bathroom and found a bloody washcloth draped on the side of the bathtub. She thought about confronting her sister about her suspicions. Thought about demanding she go to the hospital. Thought about tearing Toby Jackson to shreds with her bare hands. But she hadn't. Instead she prayed Savannah eventually spilled the details of the confrontation with him and prayed she'd fended off a woman's worst fear. Then she prayed Toby Jerome Jackson was found dead the next day.

"What did Toby do?" Georgia gently inquired once her sister's tears subsided.

Savannah hesitated. Georgia knew when she hesitated that long, she more than likely wouldn't say. She'd spent years hoping Savannah might trust her enough to finally tell her the events of that night. She baby-stepped into the subject, whispering, "You know you can tell me anything and I'll keep it safe."

Savannah looked away and hugged Georgia tight again, "I can't tell you this."

"Did he rape you?" The words begged to be spoken. For eight long years Georgia worried over the question. Pandora was out of the box now. At first she cringed at the blunt sounding inquiry. Rape. There were no softer words for such a heinous act. There was no easy way to ask except do it quick and hope for the best. But she felt Savannah stiffen. "Please tell me, Savannah. I've worried ever since that night."

"You'll tell Seth."

"I won't if you don't want him to know."

"This is not a topic I want to discuss right now."

"You haven't told a soul in all these years. It's not healthy to keep this kind of secret. You can trust me, you know that. Please don't shut me out again."

Georgia held her breath, waiting. Praying her sister would tell her at last. She gave her a squeeze, whispering, "Please tell me."

"He *tried* to rape me," she stated with firm emphasis on *tried*. "He nearly succeeded too."

When the weight of the words finally registered, Georgia swore the air vacated her lungs all at once. Tried was bad enough but at least Savannah was spared the horror of the actual act.

A familiar emotion floated to the top of her brain. Rage. For the duration of Savannah's relationship with Toby, Georgia felt only molten rage toward him. They'd met at a bar and seemed happy enough at first. Then the bruises appeared, her sister's mood darkened. Then she discovered Toby was not only following her and becoming increasingly more possessive, he was cheating on her.

Now Georgia literally wanted to kill him. If the opportunity arose, she'd show Toby Jackson the true meaning of pain.

Like her sister, Georgia felt tears welling in her eyes. She'd always admired Savannah for her strength but her respect deepened now. It took courage for any woman to admit to such a vicious attack but for Savannah it practically devastated her to disclose a moment's vulnerability.

Georgia's arms tightened around her sister, "I'm so sorry, honey. I figured when you never told me, the very worst had happened. You never would tell me anything about that night."

"You'd have told Seth then Toby wouldn't have survived the night."

"Not between Seth and me, he wouldn't have. So you fought him off?"

Savannah nodded, "It was the hardest thing I've ever done. He was so strong. I've had nightmares about it for years.

Now I'm reliving it all over again." Tears formed again and Georgia shushed her while allowing her own tears to fall. Savannah pulled back, regained enough composure to look her squarely in the eyes with a warning, "You can't tell anyone. Promise me."

Georgia promised. Telling Seth or their father would do nothing except break the trust between the sisters. That's one thing Georgia would never do.

4

Savannah had been at work just long enough to check her phone messages. She cringed when Toby's voice surfaced from her voice mail, "Hey gorgeous, just checking in to see if you know anything. Give me a call, okay?"

As an act of sweet revenge, she stabbed the delete button with great pleasure. She'd call him all right. In her search for Lori, she'd called every Savannah hotel and come up empty. Lori didn't go to the convention and obviously hadn't planned on going. There were no reservations in her married or maiden name. Either Lori lied to Toby or Toby lied to Savannah, the latter currently being Savannah's top choice. The man possessed no conscience.

Forget the slogan "Don't Drink and Drive", she thought. Toby Jackson should have been the poster child for never drinking in the first place. Do not drink, do not step over the threshold of a bar and do not, under any circumstance, let this man into your life. She done all three and paid the price. Four long years she soaked herself in Jack Daniels. The one with

Toby had been a free for all, drinking for the hell of it, or trying to kill the pain of his brutality. She was so stupid back then, she told herself, but also very lonely. After her mother's passing, she felt left behind and needed someone to hold her. Enter bar, consume drinks, meet Toby and the rest was history.

Savannah sat at her computer and brought up a records search. Her fingers finished typing Lori's name when a deep voice materialized behind her right shoulder, "Hey, sugar. I already did that for you."

She jerked rod straight, curious if that snap in her back might now be a pesky muscle strain. Massaging it, Savannah swiveled to face Ennis. Granted, her expression was less than pleasant but neither was having a person sneak up on her. From here on out I'm naming him Ennis the Menace, she vowed.

"Your back hurting today?" he reached around to, she assumed, rub it for her.

"Not until a moment ago," she blocked his hand. "Quit ambushing me, Ennis. It's not nice." The aggravation eased somewhat to her relief. She decided to move her computer to face the door that day or Ennis would scare into a dislocated disc or worse.

"Sorry," he apologized then stepped back, a frown wrinkling his brow. "You really look like hell this morning."

Before allowing her jaw to drop in shock, Savannah answered, "Well, at least I know they don't pay you to be *nice* to me."

Ennis placed a folder on her desk, "Georgia called me this morning. She's worried about you."

Savannah glanced away. Memories of the previous night flooded her consciousness, "She say why?" She knew Georgia wouldn't expose her secret but she wanted to know *how* she'd phrased her concern. She shouldn't have disclosed Toby's attempted assault but carrying the enormous weight for eight years finally drained her of barriers to hide it behind. The insufferable nightmares plagued her on and off through the years. She'd hoped they'd disappeared forever but last night proved otherwise – in a violent way. Georgia would sport a bruise on her back for at least a week thanks to Savannah's flailing about in bed.

"She doesn't trust this Toby character and frankly, neither do I. She wants me to stick to you like Velcro..."

"I don't need a bodyguard, Ennis." She sighed, then readjusted in her seat and forced a smile, "My sister worries too much."

"Not necessarily. Have you seen what this fella searches the internet for?" He opened the folder, "Look."

One glance at the folder's contents slacked her jaw

gaping wide. He charged hundreds of dollars to "Good Vibrations", "Leather Locker", and "Forbidden Pleasures". Five hundred just to the "Leather Locker" alone. "I wonder what cost five hundred dollars," she pondered aloud.

"Don't ask."

That tweaked her curiosity, "What did he buy?" She saw him blush and nearly smiled. The only thing stopping her was the knowledge that if Toby bought restraints he could follow through on a woman what he'd started with her. No way to kick his teeth out if his victim's feet were tied down. The thought raked a chill down her back.

Ennis shook his head, "You *still* don't want to know. I'll only say leather isn't the only thing they sell. They have an interesting line of furniture that you won't find at the local Ethan Allen." He blew out a breath, "Suffice it to say, your ex is one twisted little puppy. Be glad you're not together."

"Every day," she agreed and looked at the other charges on the sheet. Then the oddity of it struck her, "Wait a minute, how did you find out? Did you just ask him and he blurted it out like he'd bought a Toyota?"

Her partner darkened to a sweet shade of plum now, "Pretty much. He's a bit too forthcoming with his information. In fact, he's as full of wind as a corn-eating horse." Ennis curled his lip, "He gave me pointers on what women like in the way of sex toys."

"Did he now?" Savannah leaned back with a demure expression, "And what would they be?"

"Savannah, stop torturing me. The guy's a pervert. I don't need sex toys to satisfy a woman..." his voice trailed off as he realized how it sounded. "Well, I haven't had any complaints, I'll say that."

Letting her vision roam his physique from head to toe, she allowed an easy smile to surface then swiveled back to the computer, "I'll just bet you haven't, big boy."

Ennis sidled up behind her, leaned to her ear, lilting, "That sounded like a challenge. Care to join me for a test drive sometime?"

Savannah thought. She was never keen on mixing business and pleasure. If getting cozy with one's partner didn't spoil a friendship and work relationship, she'd consider it, but since it did...

Ennis brushed her hair aside and pressed a soft kiss at the nape of her neck. Her breath caught in her throat. Oh, that is *so* not fair, she moaned to herself. He was playing dirty and breaking all the rules now and damn it, it was working. His lingering, persuasive kiss warned her that Ennis Rutherford was trouble with a capital T. Then her treacherous thoughts went straight to the bedroom with images of how that lingering, persuasive kiss might feel in other places....

Her typing slowed to nil and she started to turn in her seat. Ennis, however, held her still, his hands holding her shoulders, the fingers kneading the muscles.

"Ennis," she inadvertently moaned, "this isn't right." Yes, it is, her mind goaded, and you *like* it.

He leaned in again, this time caressing her ear with his warm breath, "Feels right to me." He pressed his lips to her nape again, his hands caressing down her arms to softly close around them.

She had to access the very core of her self-control to pull free of his spell. She'd never realized Ennis possessed feelings for her. She never realized she *wanted* him to have feelings for her either. Sure, he'd teased her but until then had made no overt amorous gesture. When he did that morning, though, he made it count. His kiss fluttered her stomach in a way she hadn't experienced, well, ever. As though he sensed the reaction, he pressed yet another kiss to her neck, this one on her left side, and lingered there.

Savannah drew in a breath but heard it escape unsteadily. It was time to end the little tryst before someone barged in on them. She attempted to pull away only to have Ennis tighten his hold, a sign he wasn't near finished.

Even with his gentle hold Savannah felt trapped. She'd

never been a fan of men holding her this way. She felt restrained, vulnerable. The aversion developed with Toby and carried over into any relationship she delved into. As a result, her date never quite understood her apprehension or growing panic, and they soon parted ways.

Within seconds, images of helplessness from deep within her subconscious barreled to the forefront like a runaway train. She withdrew from his touch with a little too much insistence, "We need to get back to work. Did you check his other credit cards?"

Confused, Ennis replied, "Didn't have time. Hey, what just happened? Did I do something wrong?"

Trying to clear her mind and cover her unintended kneejerk reaction, Savannah shook her head, "We're at work. Someone will catch us and Josh is a stickler about inappropriate behavior."

She knew Ennis was skeptical of her explanation. He understood their captain gave Savannah a lot of leeway on things. Josh had been good friends with her and Georgia for several years so using him as an excuse probably didn't fly with her partner but she couldn't help it. The memories and the stress overwhelmed her and she would die before telling him what Toby did to her back then. Telling Georgia proved more difficult than she ever thought. She regretted doing it too.

Burdening her sister with such powerful news wasn't right. It was Savannah's cross to bear, not Georgia's but her sister would carry it, nurture it and if the opportunity arose, Georgia would strike out at Toby. *Like you're any different*, she chided herself. If she had a chance to bury Tobias Jackson, she'd do it and sell tickets to the event. Toby hadn't succeeded that night several years ago but his actions continued to haunt her. And if presented with a means of returning a fraction of the pain he furnished her, she'd take it.

Ennis's puzzled frown deepened – she saw it from the corner of her eye – and he scratched his head.

Feeling positively stupid now, she felt the need to at least say, "Just don't grab me from behind like that. Makes me crazy in a bad way."

The lines between his eyes smoothed. She hadn't shot him down, his expression seemed to say. He nodded with a tiny smile, promising, "I'll remember that."

She busied herself flipping through the charges in the folder, "Are these all the cards they have?"

"It's all I found. They have a strange way of conducting their lives. Each card is designated for one thing. One for groceries, one for gas, one for utilities."

She studied one page with charges strictly from B & W Supermarket and another with only utilities like Cobb County

Water, Georgia Power and BellSouth.

He pointed to the Leather Locker bill, "This is their 'hobby' card."

"Hobby?"

"His word, not mine. All the toys and weird sex stuff are on this one."

"What about a vacation card?" She thumbed through the other pages, "I don't see one of those. If she had gone to the convention – which she didn't go to, by the way – there would have been charges for airlines or rental cars, food, something. Still, she's not at home. It's difficult to live on only cash when you're away from home."

"Not safe, for sure, and you'll eventually run out of green."

"There should be bank withdrawals or credit card charges somewhere."

"Want me to call him again and see what's up?"

"No. Get a court order then we'll contact the credit card companies. While you're doing that, I'll call him and find out if the son of a bitch is lying to me again. Maybe she had private cards she didn't trust him with."

"Can you blame her? I'm sure she didn't realize she was marrying the founder of Perverts R Us. When he'll spend five hundred big ones on a silly chair…"

"He bought a chair?" she inquired incredulously. "At a porn shop?"

The blood drained from Ennis's cheeks as he lifted his hand to stop her, "Please don't make me go there. It's highly unpleasant."

5

"Hiya, beautiful," Toby wrapped his arm around her shoulders and drew Savannah into a hug. Savannah pulled from his embrace almost immediately. She and Ennis decided to pay him a personal visit to look at the house and check a few other details. Plus, they assumed, Toby would feel more comfortable at home. In this case "at home" meant a swankier suburb of Atlanta, complete with gated community and streets named Manor Oaks Court and Belmore Way.

"Mr. Jackson, we've got a few more questions for you," Ennis volunteered, frowning at his presumptuous nature.

Savannah detected the irritation in his voice when Toby attempted to put his arm around her. Was Ennis jealous? And why? Hers and Toby's relationship was eight years over and she certainly didn't enjoy reliving the past, especially after the previous night's hell. If she needed to make her disdain for Toby more apparent, Ennis needed to turn in his detective's shield because he wasn't much of a detective.

Toby, dressed in gray sweatpants and black t-shirt

waved them inside. As Savannah passed him, she felt his hand at the small of her back then her hip, guiding her in. Another chill raked her spine at his touch. A brief flashed of his fingers digging into her flesh as she fought against him. Now, feeling his hand at her hip, the same panic arose and she stepped away from his touch.

Ennis moved in, blocking Toby's reach. Maybe Ennis sensed something, she thought. He certainly reacted like he did.

Toby appeared unaffected, "Something to drink? I've got coffee, tea–"

"Coffee's fine," Ennis answered, his brow still furrowed. "Black."

Toby winked at Savannah, "Coffee, gorgeous?" When she nodded, he smiled, pointing confidently at her, "I remember. Cream with a touch of sugar, coming right up."

He practically skipped from the room which allowed Ennis time to ask, "Are you all right?"

Savannah took a deep breath and released it slowly, "Yeah, I'm okay."

"But you're kinda pale…"

Toby called from the kitchen, "Have a seat, guys. Anywhere's fine. I'll bring your drinks."

Savannah noticed Ennis kept a watchful eye on her as

they sat on the large black leather sofa. Yes, he sensed something awry past a bad breakup between her and Toby Jackson.

Toby sashayed in the living room holding three cups of coffee. His hand was steady while handing each their respective cups. He stood directly in front of Savannah, his crotch in plain view.

When she looked up, she nearly choked at the thick erection making its presence known through the sweats. Toby was endowed like Catherine the Great's horse but there was no reason to push the fact in her face.

She glanced in Ennis's direction and he shifted his vision to Toby's crotch then back to Savannah. Then he leaned back and leisurely curled his arm around her shoulders. She tilted her head back to meet Toby's gaze, "Thanks for the coffee. Now you can sit down," she pointed, "over there."

He stepped back to a black leather recliner and sat down with no tension in his expression or movement, "What can I do for you?"

Ennis spoke first, "We need card statements for your wife's credit cards."

Savannah took a visual tour of the living room. The furniture consisted of the leather sofa she and Ennis sat on, two leather recliners, a glass top coffee table with a black iron frame and an entertainment center that dominated the far wall. All sat atop white carpet that ended at the threshold of a spacious kitchen. Hanging in the living room were two Picasso type paintings and Toby's and Lori's wedding picture hanging on the wall behind Toby.

Savannah could say one thing about Lori. The woman must have lured Toby with her money-making abilities because she fell a bit short in the looks department. Lori was cute but not on a scale to stroke Toby's enormous ego. Of course, neither was Savannah but she doubted the likes of Marilyn Monroe would fall short in his book. He loved to bed and beat women, no matter their level of beauty.

"I don't have her statements," Toby watched Savannah's vision roaming his abode. "She probably keeps them at work. That's what she uses her cards for."

Savannah looked squarely at Toby, "Does Lori have any physical problems or ailments?"

He shook his head, "None. She's the picture of perfect health."

"Just goes in for the yearly physical, hm?" She withdrew her leather-bound writing pad and wrote something down. She noticed that particular action drew Toby's attention more than anything. He lifted his chin to better his view of her writing. In response, she crossed her leg over her knee to prohibit his snooping.

Toby leaned back with a quiet sigh, "Yeah, a yearly. Didn't we cover this yesterday?"

"Yes, and we're covering it again until I feel warm and snug about the subject."

He arched a brow. Savannah remembered very well how to rile him. Take charge of the situation, make him feel powerless. His lips suddenly took on a wily slant, "Yes, ma'am."

"How's your financial situation? A house like this costs a bundle with mortgage, taxes, insurance and you have Sandy to raise –"

"Money's fine. Between the two of us, we're earning enough to cover two of these houses," he bragged.

She guessed he intended the statement to wound her ego. Fact was no amount of money was worth taking what Toby forced on a woman. She'd rather be dirt poor and bruise free. She flipped through the credit card sheets until settling on the Leather Locker statement, "So the numerous charges on this card aren't putting a strain on your relationship?"

Nettled now, Toby plucked the sheet from her offering hand. He scanned it then smiled at her, "Not a chance, beautiful. Lori's right beside me when I place these orders. She approves of every purchase."

Savannah felt Ennis squirm, his arm pulled her closer. She glanced at her partner whose mouth now screwed to the side, a habit he had when curbing an impulsive comment.

She forged on, "So do you get frequent flyer miles or preferred buyer discounts at this Leather Locker? You spend more there than I get for a month's salary."

"They give discounts to their best customers, yes."

Now there's a club I'm glad I'm not a member of... "Toby, did you buy something from this place that scared the bejeesus out of her? When you showed it to her, she ran screaming out of the house?"

The question caused a belly laugh from Toby. He struggled to hold his coffee cup steady until finally placing it safely on the coffee table, his eyes misty from laughing so hard, "No, babe. That would be you, not Lori. She's very open-minded to this lifestyle."

Savannah felt the blood rush to her face. The blush not only tinged her cheeks scarlet but her temper as well. Ennis, sensing this, gave her a reassuring squeeze and took over, "Mr. Jackson, Savannah is doing this out of the goodness of her heart. If you insist on maintaining this attitude, I'll make damn sure this good deed ends right now."

Toby somehow sensed the degree of Ennis's temper. The detective leaned forward as if to stand, his hand on Savannah's arm to urge her into following. Toby scrambled to salve the wound, "I apologize. Sometimes it's difficult to remember we're not together, you know?" He waited for any form of acknowledgement from Savannah but there was none.

She steeled herself. Toby had a unique way of cozying up to her once he'd screwed up but today she refused to let her guard down, "Do you want your wife found? If you do, I'll do what I can. Otherwise, I'm leaving."

"What other questions did you have, sweetheart?" His voice turned apologetic. "Ask me anything, I've nothing to hide."

"What hobbies does she have?" Savannah didn't care to honestly *know* any of this information – it just served as routine questions dealing with a missing person. She wasn't sure if taking this case was her brightest moment of intellect – in fact, she was sure it wasn't – but if nothing else she'd try for the kid's sake.

"No hobbies, really. She is into the breast cancer awareness thing, though. Does that count?"

"We're not playing Scrabble, Tobias. Is that the only leisure activity she has?" Quite frankly, Savannah doubted it. People had their soapboxes but they also had real diversions, less stressful ones, that they occupied their time with. Unless Lori Jackson delighted on the stress of raising money for breast cancer awareness, she possessed another pastime.

"It's an admiral cause, don't get me wrong," she backpedaled then added, "but most people paint, read, garden, make scrapbooks, *something* else besides fundraising."

Toby sipped his coffee thoughtfully. His large hands cradled the cup as he racked his brain for an answer. Then, "Nope. Work, breast cancer awareness, me and Sandy. That's all she's got."

Savannah scribbled a note, still skeptical, "She a workaholic?"

"Eh," he gave a nonchalant shrug, "I guess so. She stays longer at work than I do. Makes more money than me too."

That's not surprising... "So, in the meantime, who's raising Sandy?"

Toby locked vision with her, his dark eyes narrowing at her curt inquiry. He leaned forward and rested his elbows on his knees, the fingers of one hand covering the balled fist of the other. "*We* are raising our daughter, Detective Prince. Now are we going toe to toe here, beautiful, or are you getting to the pertinent questions?"

Ennis leaned forward in his seat as well, "She is asking pertinent questions. We have to know as much about your lifestyle as possible to give us an idea of where your wife is."

Toby's vision didn't stray from Savannah, "Or are you

thinking of siccing the Child Protective Services mutts on us?"

"Where does Sandy spend her daytime hours?" Savannah pushed, her expression grim.

"At the neighbor's," he shot back. "Wanna run a background check on them too?"

She wrote the answer down, "Stop giving me ideas, Tobias."

Toby's hand flew to the leather writing pad, his fingers firmly gripping her wrist, "Find my wife, Savannah. Don't pick my life apart just because you're bitter over something I did."

"If you do not release me this instant, I'll take your ass in for assault." She wanted to flinch but held herself in check. He gripped her wrist with such force the tips of his fingers dug into her flesh. Resisting the urge to look away, she waited him out until he released her. Then she finished, "You came to me for help, that's what I'm doing."

She observed the muscles of his jaw clench and release a few times. When they were together, that little sign warned her to back off or be slugged. Now, however, she persisted in her mission to find his wife and if, in the process, she made him thoroughly miserable, tough.

Small flames of color slashed his handsome cheeks, "You've got a weird definition of 'help', sweetheart. Next question."

"How is your intimate relationship faring? Long hours at work, a child with needs and wants – it's got to be stressful."

Toby's body tensed as if to stand but Ennis called him down, "Stay put, Mr. Jackson, and answer the question."

Her ex seethed in the chair, his foot tapping the floor to work off excess energy – the energy he wanted to hit her with, she knew that. She watched him scrub his jaw and level a judging glare at her. After a few moments, he answered, "Our intimate relationship is fine. We are creative and habitual about sex. In fact, since you want to know *everything* about us, come here." He stood up and extended his hand to her.

Savannah did not accept the offer. Instead, Ennis asked the obvious question, "Where are you taking us?"

"The basement." Toby took her hand anyway, clasping it firmly. He tugged her to her feet and began leading her through the living room and down the hall.

Savannah threw a panicked glance over her shoulder then sighed with relief at the sight of Ennis following immediately behind. His stern expression warned of an explosion if Toby continued goading them.

Savannah pulled on her hand, "What's in the basement? Bodies?"

Toby tossed an unsavory grin back at her, "Not yet."

Now Ennis sidled behind her, his hand on her waist. She

hadn't felt this trapped in years. A fine sheen of perspiration broke out across her forehead and face. Her breathing quickened as did her heart. She hated being in small areas. Basements were underground – another problem with her – and almost always small. Adding to her anxiety were the two men sandwiching her between them. Toby, with his sleazy sexual desires, probably wanted to torture her by leading her into such a minuscule, enclosed hell. Ennis, being protective of her, closed the space between them but only managed to amplify the panic growing inside her mind.

The pressure in her chest felt crushing and her heart hammered against her ribs. Her lungs constricted until she found herself barely short of hyperventilating. Savannah told herself to concentrate on the walls, the carpet, anything to ease her distress.

The carpet was cotton soft, she thought while being dragged by the hand. It was very clean too, especially since white carpet was notoriously hard to keep. At least if she fainted the landing wouldn't be too rough. She glanced up at the paneled hallway walls. Few pictures hung and nary a one of family. The only picture gracing the wall was, again, the couple's wedding portrait, just a different pose. Suddenly Savannah's head cleared a bit. Where were the pictures of Sandy? If she had a child, pictures of the kid would weigh down the walls until they threatened to collapse.

She looked back at Ennis who frowned, "You're looking pale again," he whispered. "You feeling okay today?"

No, she felt green to the gills with dread and up to her armpits in confusion. Nothing about Toby Jackson made sense. His wife was missing yet he came onto Savannah like a single stud looking for a hot night. He should be more forthcoming with his information about his wife but he held every tidbit out of reach, making her ask questions and earn the answers. They both supposedly loved their daughter except there was no real evidence they had a child in the house. She nodded to Ennis to reassure him she was fine then realized he still didn't believe her then asked Toby, "Where is Sandy's room in this labyrinth anyway?"

"Are we dancing that dance again? I'll show you after you see the basement." His words sounded harsh now, impatient. He tugged her along by the hand and again threw an irritated glare at her, "We didn't just rent a kid and play Happy Family on weekends, Savannah. She's ours *and she's staying with us.*" The emphasis on the last few words had the impact of a load of anvils being dumped on her head one by one. For that amount of fervor, she'd expect more doting in the respect of baby pictures on walls or framed photos sitting on the furniture.

"I didn't doubt she was yours, Toby. The kid has your

eyes and your smile. I just hope she didn't inherit your temper." What she failed to locate was a hint of Lori in the child. Kids almost always favored one parent or another – Toby in this case – but besides sharing the same gender, there was truly no resemblance to Lori. Just another thing Savannah shook her head about. She hated to think Toby's genes were *that* potent.

They approached a wooden door with a deadbolt lock. He slid the deadbolt back then reached atop the door facing and retrieved a key that he slipped in a second lock. When he twisted the lock, a distinct snap echoed in the silence. He saw Savannah give Ennis a questioning glance and raised a brow himself, "What's wrong, beautiful? Afraid of the dark?"

Before she could answer, he divulged with utter vicious glee, "Oh, that's right. You're claustrophobic."

Bastard, she fumed. *Damn you for mentioning it* and *for making it sound so trivial.* It wasn't just claustrophobia. She'd been diagnosed as clinically claustrophobic. There was a difference and neither could be entirely overcome, especially by wishful thinking or closing one's eyes and thinking about something else.

Toby switched on the basement light, "Betcha didn't know that about your partner, did you, Detective Rutherford?"

Ennis didn't know however being on his toes was one of

his best traits and he replied, "She handles the condition fine in my opinion."

Savannah inwardly thanked Ennis for his discretion. She also noticed his hand covered her shoulder and gently squeezed. She took the motion as a supportive gesture since they began descending the stairs.

They were halfway down when Savannah gleaned the initial view of the "basement". The sight stopped her cold which allowed Ennis to accidentally bump her from behind. He leaned to her ear, "You need out of here?"

Yes, she thought to herself, *and I'd like a rocket strapped to my back to expedite my departure...* Savannah swallowed but her mouth felt dry as cotton. She also forced herself to shake her head no in response. No, she needed to see the depth of Toby's perversion. What she hadn't expected was a baptism of fire.

Toby descended stair by stair as though he kept something benign like a model railroad downstairs. At the bottom he turned and offered his hand to her again. As safe as she felt with him, he might as well have pointed a loaded gun at her. She wouldn't take his hand if the house was on fire and he was her only hope for survival. More than likely, she knock him down and *climb over him* to save herself.

Savannah's vision narrowed at him. Disgust turned her stomach, and for the millionth time in her life, she was grateful

Tobias Jackson was part her past and not her present.

Toby waved her to him, "Come on, gorgeous. To judge me you need to see everything, even this. If you're uncomfortable for any reason, just look around and go back upstairs." He glanced at Ennis, "We men can discuss the room at length, can't we, Detective?"

Ennis squirmed again. This time, though, his crotch bumped the small of Savannah's back as he shivered and she turned partway around. His hand squeezed her shoulder once more with a whispered, "Sorry."

Savannah knew Ennis was a good guy. He'd been nothing but proper and respectful to her since they met. When she leaned against the railing to let Ennis pass, he patted her arm and she smiled a little, hoping he understood she wasn't offended.

"What's the meaning of bringing us down here to see *this*?" Ennis inquired with a curled lip.

"This" turned out to be a veritable bondage and S & M carnival. From her vantage point, Savannah saw shelves lined with all manner of instruments for the "alternative lifestyle" as it was called. Along the back wall were various types of restraints bolted into the wall. Toby had them all. Scattered around the room were pieces of furniture – as Ennis said earlier – that wouldn't be found at the local Ethan Allen store.

Savannah's brain contracted painfully inside her skull. This creature, she reflected with revulsion, was once her boyfriend. Now she feared him to a degree that matched the night he attacked her.

He stood proudly describing each toy, each stick of bizarre kinky furniture as though they were trophies. Clearing most of the uneasiness from her voice, Savannah stated, "It's a good thing you have a lock on that door. I'd hate to think Sandy might stumble into this nightmare." The thought of that happening drained the blood to her toes. The room spun briefly until she grasped the railing harder and braced her other hand on the opposite wall. Toby could have easily killed his wife with these – these – *things*. And God only knew the danger Sandy might be in. She forced herself further down the stairs. The room could hold a key to finding Lori – at least she hoped it did. She only prayed the woman was alive at this point.

Looking around, she didn't see the infamous chair Ennis mentioned earlier so she asked Toby about it.

Never happier, Toby strutted across the room with a smile of satisfaction. It verged on arrogance, she noticed, but also faded when Ennis stopped him, "I strongly advise you not to show that thing to her."

"Oh, really?" Toby's vision cut to Savannah then back to her partner, "And if I do?"

Ennis's expression darkened and his hands went to his hips, "I'll be sorely tempted to hurt you."

Toby considered the warning. Then, humor lighting his eyes, he turned to Savannah and shrugged, "A higher authority intervened. Sorry, gorgeous. I wanted to show you though."

She glanced at Ennis whose posture remained the same. She waved it off, "Doesn't matter. If you need things like that to make sex worthwhile, you need a damn shrink." She directed her next comment to Ennis, "No wonder Sex Crimes is whining about no time off. People like him keep 'em hopping."

Toby threw his hands up in defeat, "God, you haven't changed. Still Holier Than Thou like your sister and brother. No wonder you're not married."

"If you're the best the male species can offer, yeah, no wonder I'm not. Besides, I like men with their equipment between their legs, not on a shelf."

Ennis toyed with a chain restraint, "Hey, here's an idea. Maybe the boss will let us install these in the interview rooms. We might get faster results."

Pursing her lips in disgust, Savannah hitched her thumb at Toby, "Doubt it. Some people might enjoy it too much." She walked to the shelf she originally planned to investigate - a shelf filled with a vast collection of alternative lifestyle DVDs but she wasn't looking for adult porn. People like this, this deep into the lifestyle, might dive into child porn as well. Once the rush from tormenting adults lost its luster, they sometimes looked to the younger, more vulnerable people. "For God's sake, Toby, did you buy every porn DVD made?"

He swung behind her, basically pinning her between him and the shelf, knowing how uncomfortable it would make her. "Actually, I'm finicky about my porn. I really enjoy those with spanking," he punctuated his statement with a firm swat to her bottom.

Savannah spun to face him, "Touch me again and you'll lose that hand." The longer she dealt with Toby the happier she was they weren't together anymore.

He leaned in, closing the space between them, "Handcuffs too?"

It was a struggle keeping her control. Her nostrils flared and she took a deep breath, "Push me, Tobias. Just push me." She dangled the cuffs in his line of vision. His eyes cut to them then back to her, his lips a whisper from hers, "I love to push you, gorgeous. You get fiery when you're pissed off. We had some of our best sex when you got fiery."

"That what happened to Lori? You get her all fiery then slap her down with one those sadistic... *implements*? Did you hurt her, Toby? Did you kill her?"

The impromptu interrogation stopped Toby temporarily.

He stared into her blue eyes, searching for fear but Savannah knew better than to show it.   She straightened her back, showing him she wasn't afraid.

"You know I'm not capable of murder, Savannah," he murmured.

"I know you're capable of plenty. Did you kill her?"

"Of course not!"

"I called the Westin and every hotel down there. Lori had no reservation anywhere in town. Not under her married or maiden name. You said she called you three days ago. Was it from her cell phone or a pay phone?"

Toby shrugged with a very convincing clueless expression, "Dunno. I didn't look."

"I'll get her phone records and find out. I need her cell number. I tried calling you for it last night but you didn't answer."

Toby rattled off a number from memory. Savannah retrieved her cell phone from her belt and dialed. From the corner of her eye she saw Toby fidget, his palm scrubbing his jaw and chin. To Savannah, it was a telltale sign he was getting nervous and fast.

"What's that?" Ennis asked, his head cocked at an angle. From his intense expression, it looked like he strained to hear something far away.

Savannah lowered the phone. The muffled sound of "Sweet Home Alabama" rang softly in the distance – from deep within the confines of Toby's house. "Find that phone," she ordered.

They trio headed upstairs. The song rang again just as they entered the master bedroom. Savannah held Toby aside while she opened a dresser drawer. The noise rang louder. Ennis slipped on a latex glove from his jacket and burrowed his hand into the underwear drawer. "Sweet Home Alabama" finished out one last time and Savannah clicked off her phone. She turned to Toby whose eyes widened to saucers. He shook his head at her stern appearance, "Hey, whoa. That's as much a surprise to me as to you. I thought she'd taken it with her."

"You never called your wife's cell?" she asked accusingly. "Even before you came to me for help?"

"I never bother her on business trips. If she calls, fine. But I don't bother her because she doesn't like it."

"You're not making sense, Toby. Explain it in terms I can understand. You marry a woman, have a child with her and when she's missing you don't call her cell phone but call your ex-girlfriend instead. There's something wrong with this situation and I'm betting it's because you're lying to me."

6

Toby's jaw clenched so hard Savannah saw the muscles in his jaw and temple throb in harmony. His fists balled at his sides, the arms wanting – with a desire so intense she could feel it – to pull back and slingshot his knuckles right into her jaw.

"If I was a mother," she continued in the same tone, "I'd take my cell phone with me just in case something happened to my child. Plus, it's just more convenient to have rather than use a hotel phone or pay phone. Why did Lori leave it here buried in *your* underwear drawer?"

"I don't know," the words ground from between clenched teeth.

"I'll tell you something, Tobias. Mothers who give a damn about their kids do not do that. She either doesn't love Sandy like a mother should or you've taken this twisted lifestyle to its very brink. If it's the latter, I'll get a warrant to search your property and I'll uncover all your dirty, nasty secrets."

Ennis urged her back a few steps, "Easy, sugar," he mumbled. "Don't poke at him anymore."

Savannah knew it. That was partly the reason she goaded Toby. Get his temper boiling mad and he'd say something to incriminate himself. At worst, she figured, he'd yell or slap the hell out of her. He'd be stupid to flat out hit her in front of Ennis so she felt relatively safe about that, "I'll dig up your garden, disassemble your car, whatever is required to find her, to prove you hurt her. Because if you'll do it to me, you'd do it to her and you'd do it to Sandy."

Toby's vision narrowed to slits. He moved forward, growling, "I've never hit my daughter."

"But you've hit Lori, haven't you? That's one step away from child abuse and hitting is just one definition of assault."

Toby pulled his fist back and swung just as Ennis grabbed Savannah around the waist and jerked her backward. A crushing blow across the chin spun her and disoriented her but she clung to Ennis for support. Her knees caved to the sheer amount of pain and if Ennis hadn't been holding her, she'd have collapsed on the floor. Tears stung her eyes as she cradled her jaw, the faint taste of blood coating her tongue.

She'd seen it coming and lacked the speed to duck the blow. Now, as her equilibrium tilted her off-balance and her stomach rolled with nausea, she thanked Ennis for pulling her back. Sustaining the full impact of Toby's attack would've shattered her jaw, she was sure of it. Frankly, being punched in the jaw by her ex *hadn't* been seriously considered. She'd intended to spark his temper enough to engage his mouth, not his fist. Get him talking and he'd spill whatever knowledge he had about Lori's disappearance.

Ennis reinforced his embrace as she tried standing on her own. She supported herself on Ennis's arm and the dresser next to them, a pure guttural groan emerging as she did.

Toby stood motionless, the rage still pulsing through his body, "You asked for it, Savannah, and if you open your damn mouth again, I'll break it."

Ennis ensured she was sturdy enough to stand before leveling his anger on Toby. One hand encircled her ex's thick wrist and Ennis twisted him around then shoved him against the wall, "You're under arrest. You have the right to a good old-fashioned ass-kicking. You have the right to have a priest and/or an EMT present at the time of the ass-kicking. If you don't have a priest, one will be appointed free of charge to read you your last prayer. One word, Tobias Jackson. One lousy friggin' word falls outta your mouth, and I'll rip you in half myself." He snapped cuffs on Toby in record time, read him the actual Miranda Rights then turned his attention to Savannah, "You like to push your luck, don't you?"

She ran her tongue – which felt strangely numb – around her teeth. She breathed a sigh of relief when they all appeared undamaged. She nodded in a way that assured Ennis she wasn't truly suicidal but just foolish for pushing Toby so hard.

"You need to see a doctor? That was a powerful wallop."

No shit, she wanted to say. *You shoulda been on this end of it.* Instead, she settled on mumbling a weak, "No."

"Then you'd best keep quiet until we get him locked up, read me?"

She nodded, still trying to realign her jaw. She backed against the wall to brace herself. During their relationship, Toby hit her with frequent regularity, most times only enough to stun her into temporary submission. The repercussions of this attack, however, would stick around for weeks and she'd need a powerful painkiller to knock the pain reverberating in her head. If she had any doubt of his intent, he cleared it up by finishing, "If you screw around with my daughter, I'll kill you, Savannah. She's mine and she's staying with me."

"Shut up, asshole," Ennis promptly slammed him face first into a set of wooden shelves, bopping Toby's forehead hard enough it left a print of the shelf in his flesh, and nearly sent an angel statue toppling to the floor.

Toby cringed as he turned, "I'm filing brutality charges against the two of you."

"Go ahead," Ennis growled. "I'll bet assault on a police officer trumps your charge, at least with your gatekeeper." He wrapped his fist in Toby's collar, making the t-shirt constrict around his throat, "Time to get your picture taken, pretty boy. We'll see how popular you are in lock-up tonight."

7

After returning to the station, Savannah busied herself with calling Lori's parents and sister while babying her jaw with an ice pack. Ennis not only brought a Ziplock bag full of ice from the break room's refrigerator but a stern warning for her to stay away from Toby. She happily had done so. That's when she began making phone calls that gleaned no new information regarding Lori. The parents last heard from her weeks ago, the sister only a week before her disappearance. She'd called the neighbor babysitting Sandy and asked her to take care of the girl until Savannah could make other arrangements. The neighbor agreed to keep Sandy for however long she needed. That relieved stress for Savannah on one front at least.

"Who's the guy in lock-up with the 'L' on his forehead?" The voice belonged to John Mathis, a fellow detective in his early forties.

Savannah looked up, careful not to aim her jutting jaw at him. Her dignity hurt enough without John's two cents. They were friends however his personality leaned to the caustic side.

He spouted whatever came to mind, politically correct but mostly not. His indifference showed in his attire at times. The ties on his sometimes rumpled suits almost always slanted a bit to the left. He was overweight, overly opinionated and overly eager when it came to Georgia's home-baked goodies. Until her sister began bringing a separate plate for Mathis, Savannah resorted to locking her desk drawer for her cookies and brownies.

"Name's Tobias Jackson," she answered, watching him lift his glasses from his nose to the top of his head. He'd walk around then forget where they were until someone reminded him. Among the officers and detectives, she did the lion's share of the reminding... She continued, "His wife is missing and now I'm not sure whether I'm looking for a missing woman or a body. Why?"

"What'd you arrest him for?"

Savannah swallowed her pride, turned to face Mathis and removed the ice pack.

The detective stepped closer, returned his glasses to his nose and flinched, "Whoa, that's gotta hurt. He did that to you?"

She nodded. Over the past hour, her jaw managed to develop a golf ball sized lump that ached worse by the minute. Her tongue didn't fit right in her mouth and she struggled to speak clearly, "He blindsided me then he sorta slipped and hit a shelf."

A shrewd grin curved John's lips, "Ah, that's the reason for the 'L' on his forehead. I thought we were branding the losers as they came in or something." He paused only a moment, "I'm sure you and Rutherford tried to stop him from, uh, slipping..."

"As hard as Toby tried to stop his fist, yes."

He dropped the subject and his grin, "You mind if I have a word with Iron Mike while he's our guest?"

She shrugged and rested her elbows on her desk, head in hand. Her jaw began aching in strong fashion again and she gingerly pressed the ice against it, "Have more than one with him. My preferred choice is three. They shall be 'life in prison' if I'm lucky. Can you arrange that, please?"

Mathis lowered his voice, "I'll try. He matches the description of a suspect wanted for sexual assault."

Savannah's attention sharpened to the point she forgot the throbbing in her face and neck, "Mind if I inquire about the victim?"

"Woman 'bout your age, name's Cassie Hillbrough. The guy raped and beat the hell out of her. I've been working the case for about two years now. Thought I'd run him past a few other women with the same complaints."

Savannah gritted her teeth, an action that unwittingly brought the throbbing back full force with a renewed energy. Mathis sensed her pain, "You need some Tylenol or something? You look kinda sick."

Sick from pain, memories and dread from the probability of an 8.0 earthquake once Georgia saw her face. She dreaded the moment any of her family caught sight of her. She shook her head, "Mathis, all I really need is Toby Jackson in prison. If we can make that happen, that's the best painkiller in existence."

8

Savannah always had a habit of trying to keep secrets from Georgia. The problem was simply this: Georgia was psychic. She could sniff out trouble better than a bloodhound, at least when it came to Savannah. That particular day's events, however, could easily be sniffed out by Stevie Wonder if he were living on Saturn. The knot on her jaw now resembled a small plum, complete with a cleft where Toby's wedding ring tattooed itself into the flesh. The level of grief it provided convinced Savannah to think twice before provoking a man that relentlessly again.

She groaned every time she opened her mouth to speak. She didn't dare touch the knot again – she'd unconsciously done that a couple of times with disastrous results so she dove into some new information Ennis dug up minutes earlier.

The phone records from Peaches Realty revealed that Toby received approximately eight phone calls three days ago. None from the Savannah area code and were, in fact, all local calls. None were from a pay phone. Instead of going to Ennis's office which would annoy her jaw further with the movement, Savannah picked up the phone, "Holmes, I've got a favor to ask."

Ennis's voice dropped to a low, suggestive tone, "And what's my lovely Watson got on tap?"

"Since you've forbidden me to call on my ex, I need you to ask him what time Lori supposedly called him three days ago."

"On my way," he agreed then hung up.

Savannah rested her head in her hands, careful not to irritate her new growth. She closed her eyes and sighed. If something didn't turn up quick on Lori's case, she'd be forced to get a search warrant for Toby's house. Just another way to make Tobias Jackson delighted with her. He'd most likely called his lawyer by now – knowing Toby he was a high-powered, high-dollar suit who made his fortune on police brutality cases. Somebody probably skillful enough to beat a murder rap if a body ever materialized. Savannah prayed Lori was okay. She'd done her share of informing families of a deceased loved one. Knowing that Lori suffered the same abuse she had years ago reinforced her fear that Toby's violence escalated with time. Abusers never stopped, they merely got older.

"Oh my God," cried an all too familiar voice.

Uh-oh... Savannah opened her eyes to see Georgia closing in on her like a hawk on a mouse. Before having time to respond, Georgia rounded her desk and tilted her chin for a better look, "My God, Savannah. This looks awful."

"It's okay, really," she tried pushing her sister's hand away only to have it return as if by magnetism. "It's really tender though, so be careful." Savannah cringed at her speech that now began taking on a Daffy Duck lisp. "What are you doing here?"

"Ennis called me."

Her lips pursed with annoyance then she relaxed when the pain bolted up her head and down her neck, "God sakes, are you having an affair or something? You two talk more than he and I do."

"Where is he?" Georgia inquired sternly.

"Who, Ennis? He's downstairs."

"Not Ennis. *Toby.*"

Savannah saw her sister's hands rolled into fists, the knuckles blanched white. Personally, she'd seen enough of that action today and didn't look forward to more, even if Toby was the victim. Georgia had killing in mind and Savannah wasn't about to let her near him. He'd hurt enough people in his life and to see Georgia behind bars for assaulting an asshole like him would destroy Savannah.

Georgia spun on her heel and headed for the door, a woman on a mission, "I'll find him myself. I know he's here because Ennis said he arrested him for hitting you."

Savannah leapt from her seat, surprisingly unaware of the pain flowing through her face. She barely caught her sister by the arm, "If you even look at Toby, you'll give *me* a rash. You're not touching him or talking to him, Georgia. Go home."

When Georgia turned, tears gleamed in her eyes, "I'm fed up with him hurting you. If someone took out their anger on him, he'd think twice about hitting you again and I'm the perfect candidate for the job."

Trying to pull her obstinate sister back into her office nearly proved impossible. Georgia planted herself for the duration and only after one good yank did she budge. Savannah tried to reason with her, "You can't go in there and beat Toby up. I'd have to arrest you, you know. Then there's those inconvenient obstacles called jail and trial to contend with. Besides, Toby slipped and fell headfirst into a shelf after he hit me."

"He what?"

"He *fell*..." she let her sentence trail hoping Georgia picked up on the meaning.

After only moments, Georgia smiled and whispered, "Did Ennis –"

Savannah nodded. Her sister laughed softly then, "Good for him. I still want to see Toby behind bars, the rotten bastard. Can I at least go look?"

"Best to avoid temptation as Mama always said. You need to go home, Georgia. I'm fine."

Georgia arched one brow, "For a squirrel, maybe. Looks like you're stocking up for winter."

Savannah didn't find the humor in her comment, "Pick on somebody your own age." She barely touched it and winced, "Seriously, it hurts like hell."

"If you'll take off early, you can stay with me. I've got some painkillers at home but you can't drive after taking them. I'll make something soft to eat too. Is it a deal?"

"If you'll go straight home and not go downstairs."

Georgia thought a moment then capitulated, "Straight home then."

"And don't tell Seth about this," she warned.

Exasperation flashed across Georgia's face as she planted her hands on her hips, "I won't have to, hon. That thing isn't going to fade until well after Thanksgiving."

Savannah shrugged, "I'll hide it with makeup."

"Oh, that'll work for sure." Her sister delicately mocked then retained a dubious tone, "Get real, Savannah. Our brother was an Army Ranger. He's slightly attuned to notice odd or different things. Right now it looks like you're hatching an egg in there and I suspect the swelling will take a while to subside. Seth's not a dummy."

"I know that. I'll tell him Toby's in prison. Maybe by then he actually will be."

9

Savannah glanced at her watch again. Only five minutes passed since she last looked. Then she sighed. Amazing how time dragged on when a person was in pain. Most times, an hour or more passed before she'd check the time. Of course having the equivalent of a hen egg in one's mouth tended to make a person not only nervous but terribly grumpy. Worst of all, Georgia was right about Thanksgiving. Unless, for some inexplicable reason, she arrived at Seth's house dressed as Don Corleone, everyone would know Savannah got whacked upside the head by her ex-boyfriend.

She looked at her watch again. Two minutes had passed. Except for waiting on an update from Ennis, Mathis, and a lab guy she had checking on a few leads, she'd ditch work and go to Georgia's for that painkiller.

Just as she'd decided to leave, Ennis sauntered into her office with a wink, "Hiya, slugger."

She smiled weakly, "I was on the other end of the fist, remember?"

"You took it well though and you didn't try to slug him back."

"I was too rattlebrained to know my own name, much less fight back," she pursed her lips. The damn Daffy Duck lisp had returned and now her tongue felt bigger inside her mouth. With any luck, she'd choke to death before quitting time, "Besides, all I managed to do was get him a night in jail."

Ennis nearly laughed. She sensed it and gave him a narrow look. "Besides" emerged "Bethides" and "was" sounded comically like "wath". He scrapped the smirk and settled for a sympathetic stance, "Perhaps more will come of today than your swollen jaw. I saw Mathis down in lock-up talking to him. Oh, and before I forget, Jackson swears the call from Lori came around 1 p.m. on Monday."

"How did you get him to swear to anything?"

A lazy grin inched across his lips, "It's amazing what being cornered by two detectives can produce. Why *is* Mathis talking to him anyway?"

Savannah avoided eye contact with Ennis, "He's a suspect in a sexual assault case. There may be more than one victim." She noticed he didn't reply even as she referred to the phone records from the realty business.

He stood a moment then quietly shut the door, "Can I ask you something personal?"

Savannah figured it was about time. Ennis pretty much shied away from her after she'd pulled back from him that morning. Doubly so since she tore away from Toby's embrace. She wondered how long it might take Ennis to ask – now she knew. "No, Ennis, I'm not gay although for all intents and purposes I *should be* after enduring a relationship with Toby Jackson."

He stopped in mid-sit, his body half-in and half-out of the only available chair, his tone revealing pure disbelief, "What?"

"That's what you wanted to ask, right? I pulled away from you earlier and basically treated Toby's touch like the plague so I can see why you're confused."

"Before you further this wild notion, that isn't what I thought. I figure I'll wear you down into having dinner with me, going to a movie, spending time together and stuff like that. And I can see why you acted that way at Jackson's house. My question was – are you one of his victims?"

Savannah's mouth snapped shut. She'd overplayed her hand and now had Ennis diving into a preciously private part of her past. He'd read her like a damn book and she *really* didn't like that. For years she prided herself on keeping her secrets just that. Secret. Now her partner read her better than her own sister.

She fiddled with the pages of the phone records. Her face flushed and merely worsened when he leaned closer. He whispered, "It isn't your fault, you know. He's a predator. And he'll pay for hurting you, Lori and every other woman he's assaulted." He reached across the desk and covered her hand with his, "He won't hurt you again."

She struggled against releasing the tide of emotion she unleashed that night at Georgia's house. Her lip quivered and she felt his hand tighten on hers. Before she melted into a stew of tears, she replied, "I'm not one of his victims in that respect. He liked to hit me though – but I got my revenge."

"That what he meant by siccing the whole department on him back then?"

Eh, not exactly, no... But, "Kind of. I'd broken up with him and he kept begging me back. When I refused, he hit me. My partner and my new boyfriend – another cop – saw it and taught him a lesson I didn't ask them to."

"I'da killed the son of a bitch," Ennis admitted. "Send his ass to God and let Him sort it out." He hesitated as if weighing his words, "If you ever want to talk or just go out and kill time or go to dinner, I'm here, you know."

Ennis's offer meant a lot to her. He wasn't pushy, domineering or arrogant. He was... just right. Probably perfect too, but she'd hold off on that decision for now, "Thanks. I might take you up on dinner soon enough."

Ennis nodded and leaned back in the chair. He waited a moment then snorted good-naturedly, "Gay. Of all the things you coulda mentioned..."

Savannah glanced up and saw his smile. Ennis possessed a very contagious smile. She noted that the first day they met. When he smiled, his whole face relaxed and sat back for the ride. An even, white set of teeth gleamed and she swore even his beautiful brown eyes grinned also. His smile encouraged one from her as he chuckled, "That's one thing, sugar, *one thing* I'm sure about. You may be a tad unbalanced sticking your face in front of a dude's fist, but you are not gay."

Embarrassed, she lowered her vision to the phone records in her hand. Her jaw pulsed again as a cheery little reminder of her stunt, "I didn't expect him to nail me. I really thought he'd use reason. You know, with two cops standing there."

"But with you pushing all his buttons, I'm surprised he stopped with one. Damn, woman, you're outright terrifying."

"I did purposefully push Toby but come on, after what he did and tried to do to me when we were together?"

He lifted a hand to halt her preaching, "I never said you were wrong. I only said you were scary. Can you restrain yourself from now on? I'd hate to tell your family you were killed by a speeding fist."

"I'll restrain my provocation of suspects if you'll stop calling Georgia and tattling on me. I swear the two of you are worse than parents."

A soft knock at the door broke the conversation. "Come in," she called. Tom Clayton, the lab guy, poked his head in, "Your hunch paid off."

Savannah waved him in her office. Tom peeked around the door to see Ennis sprawled in the chair, legs crossed and his finger casually stroking his lower lip. Savannah waved him in again – Tom was a shy one, she reminded herself. He looked sort of like Archie from the comic books. A bashful, glasses-wearing Archie.

Tom's eyes darted anxiously behind his glasses, switching from Savannah to Ennis. He took it upon himself to explain to Ennis, "You already know there are two cell phones registered to Tobias Jackson, his and the one you found at the house. But Savannah figured Mrs. Jackson might have a second cell phone, or one of her own. I checked with the phone companies and she's registered under Lori Evans with this number."

He ambled closer to her desk and handed her the phone number, "It's a completely different cell company and the bill goes to a Karen Evans."

"Her mother," Savannah volunteered.

He nodded, "I'm guessing she wanted the phone to remain a secret, at least from her husband."

"That would be a good guess," she answered while studying the number. "Wonder what calls were received on this phone. Could you –"

"Already done," Tom finally smiled. He reached in his coat and handed her a folded sheet of paper. "She's a busy lady."

Savannah eagerly opened the paper and studied it, "Indeed." Several phone calls to and from the cell phone were made days before the convention in Savannah. The calls dwindled to nothing during the convention's schedule with the exception of two.

The numbers seemed familiar to Savannah so she backtracked through the ones she had. One incoming call came from her mother and one from her sister – just that day. If her family now knew her location – or situation – why didn't they inform Savannah? She'd made sure to give each her work and cell numbers if they heard from Lori. Again, nothing about Toby's life made sense so it figured that his wife's life didn't either. She only knew Lori now realized Toby contacted the police concerning her whereabouts.

"Ever feel like people work hard to complicate your

life?" Savannah asked Ennis.

He chuckled, "Every day. But I haven't given up on you yet."

His statement threw her temporarily, drew her gaze to his and she caught his crafty grin and wink. Ennis's infectious smile effortlessly lifted the corners of her mouth. *He would be so easy to love*, she thought. He was old-fashioned, protective, charming and flirty with a good sense of humor. Not to mention he was a handsome devil, a fact Georgia pointed out the moment she first saw him.

Ennis's grin widened and he arched a brow, "I won't give up either."

Suddenly she became acutely aware of Tom's presence. His uncomfortable posture and lowered vision persuaded her to return to the phone records from Peaches Realty. At twelve fifty-two, one call went to Toby's extension at the office. "Wait. This is a local number," she mumbled. "She called him from Atlanta when she was supposed to be in Savannah."

"Curiouser and curiouser," Ennis thought aloud while he continued worrying his lower lip.

Savannah turned to her computer and entered a phone number search. It took a brief few seconds for the result to pop up on the screen. "Hmmm," was the lilted answer from her.

"That sounded inviting and indicting," Ennis offered.

"The Westin Peachtree Plaza."

"Uh-oh," Ennis nearly sang. "You reckon the missus broke Commandment number seven?"

"You mean like Toby enjoys breaking people's jaws?" She clicked off the computer then smiled, "Thou shalt not assume anything, Holmes, but the Westin seems a good place to commit adultery if one is inclined to do so."

"Not only beautiful but brainy as well, my lovely Watson. We're not doing anything else so you want to check it out?"

"You might be interested to know," another voice entered the conversation, "that new charges just came through on Mrs. Jackson's business card."

Savannah and Ennis turned their attention to Grady Portman, the resident snoop on credit cards. "Do tell," she encouraged. "We enjoy windfalls of information."

"It makes us both giddy," her partner added with a wink.

Grady ignored his statement and addressed Savannah specifically, "The charge is to Mark Zimmerman, Attorney at Law."

"Trouble in Paradise," Savannah presumed. "He's a divorce lawyer. Maybe she's not as silly as I first thought."

Grady handed her the full page report, "There's also a

charge for some swanky room at the Westin Peachtree. Room service too. She must be eating like a horse in there."

"There's enough food charged for at least two people," she noticed. Then she glanced impishly at Ennis, "Wanna go crash a party?"

He stood quickly and offered her a hand, "Thought you'd never ask."

Savannah felt a wave of relief roll through her. Maybe this case was finally coming to a conclusion. One that benefited everyone. If she was filing for divorce, Lori would be rid of Toby and Toby would be in jail for a while – hopefully a long time if the sexual assault cases panned out. And the biggest prize of all: Savannah could finally be free of her ex. Then she thought of Sandy. Well, she thought, Lori would take good care of the kid. After all she was her mother. *Yeah, and she left her behind with a creep who likes to hit women. Some mother.* The fact still nettled Savannah. It didn't make sense why a mother would do it. Before the night was finished, she vowed to have some answers. Answers that made sense, for a change.

10

The Westin Peachtree towered over downtown Atlanta, encased in a cylindrical mirrored column seventy-three stories tall. A glass elevator in a smaller attached cylinder led to a revolving restaurant and public observatory atop the building. When the old thirteen story Henry Grady Hotel was demolished and the new hotel finished construction in 1976, the people of Atlanta didn't warm to the Westin right away. Some claimed it destroyed the city's Old South charm. However, as the years passed and they saw it standing reverently in the city skyline, their dislike ebbed to tolerance then acceptance. Even now the place was considered upscale but back then Atlantans considered it not only elite but a significant statement. Some equated it the Empire State Building of the South while others still disapproved but were too polite to speak their minds.

Savannah considered the Westin an answer to her prayers, at least tonight. But getting there was the trick, especially with Ennis behind the wheel. The man drove like a madman in the Acura RSX. The car, painted Nighthawk Black, belonged only on racetracks, she decided. Not in the hands of an overzealous detective who possessed an iron stomach. Ennis turned corners, happily explaining the specs of how "perfectly" the RSX cornered. He sped down avenues and boulevards bragging about his Type S's 210 horsepower – all while she clung to the door handle *and* her lunch.

Savannah reinforced her grip as Ennis plowed around a corner. "Take it easy, Mario," she complained. "The G-forces are killing my jaw."

Ennis turned to her – another thing that worried her. How could he drive safely with his vision drawn from the street? He offered an apologetic smile, "Sorry. Just don't want the missus to fly the coop before we get there."

Her death grip expanded to two hands now, one remained on the door handle while the other went to the dashboard, "She already knows we're looking for her. Her mother and sister called her."

He slowed briefly, a welcome change to the blurring pace they'd maintained since their journey started, "Yeah, what made you think of the second cell phone?"

She shrugged, "Toby likes to keep tabs on his women. Make them check in at certain times, be available for his calls, crap like that. If I were married to the bastard, I'd want my own phone so he couldn't check the statement. That way, I could call who I wanted without Big Brother looking over my shoulder. Ennis, watch the road."

Ennis turned back and swerved around a slowing car. Savannah sighed and swallowed hard. She never should have agreed to let him drive. Bracing her hand on the dash as he swerved around another car, she threw him an annoyed frown, "You drive worse than my brother did before he got married."

Ennis laughed, "Oh, so I need a wife and I'll drive better."

"Sanely," she corrected. "You'll drive sanely."

Before making the turn onto Andrew Young Boulevard, he winked at her, "Do I hear an offer in there somewhere?"

"It could depend on whether I survive this ride or not." Savannah noticed his foot let off the gas. Even through the small waves of nausea and pain, she realized he slowed the car to a manageable speed. Perhaps she should set him straight in case he misunderstood, "Hey, I'm not proposing to you, if that's what you think."

Ennis shook his head, tickled from her statement, "Not yet, maybe. But I don't give up. Plus, I don't have a ring and I haven't spoken to your father yet."

"Stay away from my father. He doesn't accept anyone new, especially if they're marrying one of his kids. Seth is still paying for marrying Leah and Daddy hasn't accepted Matthew either. It's my decision if I get hitched anyway." She gulped when the car came to an abrupt stop.

"210 Peachtree Street. We are here." Before opening the door, he pried Savannah's hand from the dash, "While we're here, we'll book a room for our honeymoon."

She willed her other hand to open the car door. It seemed glued to the sturdy, dependable handle. Even when Ennis rounded the car and opened the door for her, her hand remained solidly fisted around the handle. Before toppling onto the pavement, she forced her hand to open, "Your ancestors were moonshiners, weren't they? That's how you can drive like that and not wreck."

"Marry me and you'll discover my fascinating ancestral past."

"If I married you, I'd probably find out you're related to Marc Antony."

He sidled up behind her and mumbled softly, "I hear he was a big, loveable teddy bear which means I probably am related. Wanna book a room and find out, Cleo?"

His offer encouraged a smile to surface, even though it hurt like the devil. But the pain didn't matter right then, "You're impossible."

They made their way past the doorman as he finished, "And I'm falling in love with the Queen of Denial. I refuse to give up on you."

She spied the front desk and angled toward it, "Then you're more likely related to George Custer. Against all odds he forged on only to meet an untimely demise."

"I'll take my chances with you. You haven't killed me yet and that's got to be a good thing."

They hiked through the spacious atrium lobby encircling the elevator core. Several people mingled around the large silver columns throughout the room. Modern art sculptures resembling large wooden eggs and genie bottles sat atop even more modern looking tables. Those were flanked by uncomfortable looking padded chairs that should have been left in the seventies with bean bag chairs. Her opinion of the carpet fell into the same garish category as it presented an overdone Persian rug effect. Looking at it made her positively dizzy. Or it could have been the hangover effects of Ennis's driving...

Savannah visually perused the people in the room, past all the families and businessmen, she searched for anyone who resembled Lori Jackson but came up empty. It was time to approach the young upstart at the desk. The skinny woman, her straight blond hair flowing past her waist, would present a problem as sure as Toby's fist made a knot on her face. Even as she and Ennis approached, the blonde seemed to sense the fact they were police and obtained a prim and proper "I can't reveal that information" stance.

Ennis recognized the movement and, along with Savannah, smiled as they displayed their badges. Savannah allowed him to break the ice, "Detectives Rutherford and Prince, Atlanta Police. What is Lori Jackson's room number?"

Sure enough, the woman shook her head with determination. Judging by her expression, it wasn't fear of retribution for revealing the information – she just clearly drew a line in the sand. She wouldn't give the room number without a warrant.

However, before she could speak, Savannah leaned across the polished maple counter, her voice low, "It's not a trick question. Give us the room number or I'll have a quaint little chat with my friend in the fire department. I'm sure the exits need checking, the sprinkler systems need approving, and with a building this size, why, it could take days. And all those fire codes – if you fail only *one*..."

"*Detective,* you *wouldn't,*" Ennis scolded. "This establishment stands to lose hundreds of thousands of bona fide U.S. dollars – if that should happen." He turned back to the desk clerk, "Now I don't know much about the hotel business but that couldn't be beneficial to your employee 401k."

The blonde pursed her lips. Her expression evolved to a frustrated scowl directed at Savannah. The detective held her badge closer for the woman to see, "Don't think I won't do it. Lori Jackson. Give her up."

The desk clerk sighed, clicked a few keys on the computer's keyboard and waited. In the meantime, it gave her time to sneer once more at Savannah who merely smiled again. A few seconds passed and the answer came, "Room 942." Then to save face and retain a sliver of control she added, "Don't ask for a passkey either."

"Does the door have a knob or handle?" Savannah inquired curtly.

The woman's patience level bottomed out, "Of course it does."

"Then we don't need a passkey. I assume she's capable of opening the door herself." Overlooking the nasty glare tossed her way, Savannah hitched her thumb at the elevator as a cue to Ennis and they marched through the lobby.

"Charming little shrew, wasn't she?" he asked in a near whisper.

Savannah agreed, "Much as I like time off work, being suspended for slapping her doesn't sound very appealing right now."

They continued toward the elevator and were nearly there when Ennis stopped her with a hand on her arm, "If you're claustrophobic, this won't be a pleasant ride. Want me to do it?"

She stared up at her nemesis. It seemed harmless enough. Just a simple elevator. But Savannah already felt her body and mind responding to the concept of being locked in a tiny box that would lift her to the heavens.

She tried to swallow back the fear as best she could, "I'll go but I'll face away from the windows. What kind of sicko made see-through elevators anyway?"

"A Yankee, no doubt."

They waited for the elevator to descend from the top floor. Looking up at the small enclosure sliding down the enormous clear tube, she felt a current of sickness creep into her veins.

The elevator finally slowed to a gentle stop in front of them and they allowed the guests to file off en masse. She noticed the majority sported gleeful smiles as though they'd taken an exciting amusement park ride. She'd never be that damn jolly over riding inside a sardine can that played dull music.

Ennis stepped in and offered her his hand, "I've got a temporary remedy for claustrophobia if you're willing to try it."

Trying to conceal the absolute panic growing inside, she accepted his hand and climbed in. To keep her mind on something other than the next few minutes, she asked, "I'm willing to try nearly anything. What is it?"

He slid his arm around her waist and drew her close while his other hand pressed the "9" on the lighted panel, "The trick is distracting you, taking your mind off where you are."

She stiffened the instant she heard the doors slide shut behind her. Now she faced Ennis, their bodies aligned together and his whiskey colored eyes staring calmly into her distressed blue ones. He pressed her closer, "Just keep your attention on me, sugar."

Now *that* was easy. His arms trapped her in a loving embrace, the heat pouring from his body, his intent gaze holding hers as gently as his arms around her. She was doomed, she thought. Doomed, but in a good way. His closeness sent her pulse racing. Her breathing quickened and though she could have attributed it to her claustrophobia, she recognized the truth. Ennis caused the arousing upheaval inside her. She wanted him to kiss her. She'd held off long enough, she told the annoying straightlaced angel on her shoulder – the one warning her against indulging in a kiss. *What happened to No Getting Involved*, it asked, shaking a finger at her. *Kissing Ennis Rutherford, enjoying his embrace will lead to trouble down the road…*

Oh, shut up, she told it just as Ennis slowly leaned down, his lips descending to hers.

Savannah felt his lips sweep hers like a soft whisper. They returned again, this time lingering. Savannah not only accepted his kiss with an eagerness that surprised him, but she promoted it by returning his embrace. The pain in her jaw that radiated down her neck didn't matter. The ground speeding away from them didn't matter. Nothing except his kiss mattered. If Ennis merely meant to distract her, he surpassed his goal. The passion in his kiss told the story. There was clear emotion involved and it encompassed her as well.

Ennis cupped the back of her head to gently hold her to the kiss. Savannah hated to tell him but it was quite unnecessary. Nothing could tear her away from him at the moment. She relaxed in his embrace, her eyes closed as they kissed. Now she wished the ride would last a few more floors – or even a few more days. She felt Ennis's hand slide down her back and nestle at her bottom. He urged her closer against his body, his throat releasing a quiet groan as he did.

A soft bell announced their arrival but neither of them seemed to hear it. Only when the doors slid open did they break the kiss, Ennis taking a deep breath and Savannah releasing a long sigh. A smile curved her lips when she looked at him. Ennis, his face flushed, flashed his own smile at her, "No offense but I hope you're just as claustrophobic going down as you were coming up."

11

Marching down the hallway, they set their sights on room 942. Savannah still felt a tingle from Ennis's kiss, still tasted him on her lips. His intentions were good but he'd stirred her in ways she didn't need right now. She didn't need the butterflies in her stomach nor did she need the foolish grin she'd acquired since their elevator ride together.

She cut her eyes to the side and noticed Ennis couldn't stop smiling either. As they approached Lori's room, Savannah gave him a quick glance, "You ready?"

Ennis nodded and she knocked on the door. They both waited for someone to acknowledge them but only heard noises inside like someone scrambling around the room. Savannah knocked again, "Atlanta Police. Open up."

A few moments passed when the door cracked open. All Ennis and Savannah saw was a blue eye swapping a narrow glance between them. "Badges, please," the woman requested.

Savannah exchanged a look with Ennis but both removed

their badges from their belts and presented them to her. Savannah spoke first, "Mrs. Jackson, we need to talk to you."

"What are your names?"

Ennis took over, "Detectives Rutherford and Prince."

Once the woman seemed convinced of their identities, she swung the door open, "What's this about?"

Stepping inside compared to exploring a disaster area. An explosion of clothes and bed sheets littered the floor and furniture. The blinds were closed – thankfully – but Savannah could see everything just fine. The bed basically looked bulldozed with the comforter tossed over the desk and chair and the sheet wadded up in the floor at the foot of the bed. "Bad night?" Savannah asked.

"I wasn't expecting company," Lori replied, displeased with Savannah's tone. She leaned down and picked up the sheet and tossed it in a corner as though it might help the room's overall appearance.

Again, Savannah marveled at Lori Jackson. The spunky golden-haired woman stood a few inches shorter than Savannah's five-nine and her frame would be described as delicate. She'd lost weight since hers and Toby's wedding picture which gave her a more fragile appearance.

Lori wore a fluffy white terrycloth Westin bathrobe and her wavy blond hair – damp from taking a shower – hung about her shoulders in a yellow Medusa's nest.   Her all-around look as Ennis might say, was a cross between "rode hard and put away wet" and "she was in the outhouse when lightning struck".

Suddenly Lori did a double take at Savannah, "Wait a minute. Detective *Prince*?" She shook her head, swinging the Medusa nest back and forth across her shoulders. "Oh great, another ex-girlfriend. You all crawl out of the woodwork around here."

Savannah jumped to the defensive, "Hey, I didn't track you down for my health, you know. Toby came to me to find you–"

"Well, you found me, honey. Now go home and tell him you didn't."

"You're supposed to be at a convention in Savannah. That's over two hundred miles off the mark. Did you make a wrong turn out of your driveway?"

Lori gave her a patronizing glare, "So sue me. You think Toby ever tried to cover his lies? The man has no scruples. He'd hump the maid in our own bed – in front of me – if the moment struck him and God knows he has *a lot* of moments."

Well, Savannah couldn't argue with that. Toby's morals rivaled those of the swingers in the 1970's. If it looked fun, do it. If it felt fun, do it again and again.

Lori gathered the robe at the collar, "Don't you find it odd that he asked *you* to find his wife?"

Yes, she did. But as usual when it regarded Toby, Savannah spent her time on automatic pilot instead of trying to analyze his motives – and once more, it seemed to snag her into his trap.

Lori sighed, "I'm filing for a divorce that he's known about for weeks. He didn't need to track me down, he's just..." she paused to measure Savannah's mood. Lori folded her arms in a protective posture, "I'm not trying to hurt anybody but he's probably searching for a replacement."

Well, that definitely stung. If Lori attempted to cut her down to size it worked if only temporarily. Savannah, though, held the ultimate trump card. She wasn't Toby's wife. Now more than ever she thanked God for that simple but essential fact. When Lori said "I do" at the alter, Savannah guessed she had no clue what contract she was signing. "And what about Sandy?" Savannah asked, "Are you filing for full custody?"

His wife shook her head, dogged in her position, "He can keep the brat."

Lori's terminology heated Savannah's temper to the boiling point. The woman recognized the fact and backpedaled, "She's not mine, Detective. He had the kid with another woman so when I married Toby, I had an instant family. I can't and won't touch her."

Savannah tried not to grit her teeth. She developed the habit as a uniform cop so she wouldn't say anything to get herself suspended. When children were involved, the move became her safety net. Today, however, she let it all hang out, "Your empathy for the child turns me positively weepy."

Lori's lips pursed. Her nostrils flared like a bull about to charge, "I *care* but she's not *mine*. What can I do? Since I married the bastard all I've heard is 'she's my daughter, I can do what I want'."

Savannah considered the words a moment. Then, as though light dawned on what they *could* mean, her brow sank and she stepped closer to Lori who perceived Savannah's posture and expression as a threat. She wasn't incorrect. "Lori, what exactly did he mean by that? That he can do what he wants?"

Intimidated, Lori shrank back now, "You think he only abused you, me and the copious rabble of girlfriends he had? No one's immune, Detective. Not even his own child."

Ennis put a hand on Savannah's shoulder. He intended the light squeeze to be a warning of caution. He knew how she felt about child abuse. An utterly despicable act on the innocent, that's how most people viewed it. But living through the hell herself, Savannah vowed to help any child in danger and destroy the person or people inflicting the abuse. Once Ennis witnessed the degree of anger in her expression, he tightened his hold as Savannah inquired, "You saw him hit her?"

Still wary of the detective's personality change, Lori nodded, adding, "I have pictures at the house of her bruises and mine but you should know there's more to his depravity than just bruises."

Ennis reinforced his hold on Savannah. Somehow he must have detected exactly what troubled her. She wouldn't put anything past Toby now. She'd learned enough about her ex over the past day to realize his degeneracy sank to the bone. If he sexually molested a child, God help him because the next time she saw him…

Ennis gave her shoulder another squeeze and attempted to lower the tension in the room, "We'll need those pictures, ma'am. You'll get them back as soon as we document the abuse and find Sandy a place to live."

Lori caught the murderous glint in Savannah's eyes and stepped back in an act of self-protection, "I tried to help her but all I got was a week in the hospital for my efforts. You know how Toby is."

It was Savannah's turn to nod. Yes, Toby could be a heartless son of a bitch but Savannah would sacrifice her own life to save a child in danger. If she'd seen Toby hit Sandy – or worse – then removing the child from the threat was foremost followed by a trip to Hurt City for Toby.

Savannah noticed Ennis staring at the night stand. His grasp on her shoulder lightened as he stepped closer to the object of his attention, "Mrs. Jackson?"

Lori turned to Ennis, readying herself for battle with the male cop now. However, Ennis merely lifted a watch, "This is a mighty fine Rolex. A bit big for someone your size though. Heavy too." He showed it to Savannah. The shiny gold watch had a thick band to match. Even from her distance she saw the diamonds surrounding the dial. She'd seen a few of these particular Rolexes during her lifetime. It was a Rolex Daytona and the men who wore them went as fast as the cars they drove. "Wow," Savannah exhaled. "That sweetheart set someone back at least eighteen grand. Who does it belong to?" She aimed the question directly at Lori with no wiggle room for hemming or hawing.

Ennis pointed to the closed door across the way, "Detective, I'm betting the answer is behind that bathroom door." He turned to face the bathroom and knocked, "Come on out."

Lori now verged on a conniption, "You can't do this. I answered your questions but this is invasion of privacy."

Savannah waved off the woman's paranoia, "Settle down. Cops have a problem about people hiding from them. Makes them think the person might have a weapon and do something stupid with it. He'd better come out before my partner takes over."

As if the person heard her warning, the door slowly opened and they saw a man's hand wave through the crack, "I don't have any weapons but I'm only wearing a towel –"

Ennis and Savannah exchanged glances again and Ennis answered him, "There's a reason they equip those rooms with towels. Come on out but keep yourself respectable. My partner's had a hard enough day."

A half-naked, broad-shouldered figure inched out of the bathroom, one hand in the air, the other securing a thick white bath towel at his waist. Savannah guessed his age about forty-five or so, his dark damp hair exhibiting a few gray streaks. He clearly worked out as his body appeared firm and muscular. One quick glance at Savannah and his gut tightened harder, his grasp solidly reinforced on his towel, "Ma'am. Sorry for not being properly dressed."

"Who are you?" she asked.

"Detective," Lori cautioned.

"Mrs. Jackson, please refrain from interrupting me. I'm conducting an investigation in case you forgot. Your," she paused to find a palatable word, "friend here might have useful information. Now, who are you?" She asked the man again.

"Mark Zimmerman, Lori's divorce lawyer."

Ennis blew out a breath, "Hell of a retainer you're giving him."

Lori recoiled at the statement but after witnessing the warning Savannah gave her, she backed up to the bed and sat down with a sigh. Savannah felt her staring at her. The moment they made eye contact again, Lori couldn't help herself, "Like Toby never screwed around on you, honey? I see he's still into the physical reinforcement, judging by your jaw."

Savannah suddenly became aware of the knot again. It hadn't throbbed since Ennis kissed her but now, since Lori and her lawyer stared at it, she wished she could camouflage it somehow. She glanced at Mark and something about his demeanor didn't set well with her. He fidgeted like Toby did when he tried to hide something from her. Her hand automatically drew back to her gun but stayed perched on the holster, "Is there a problem, Mr. Zimmerman?"

Reacting to his partner's move, Ennis not only reached

back for his weapon but drew it from its holster. He kept the .38 pointed toward the floor as the lawyer stumbled for words and shook his head.

Savannah noticed his eyes shifted to the bathroom. Now she removed her weapon as well then made her way across the room. Cautiously she padded to the door and heard Lori begin her usual protest. Ennis hushed her while following his partner.

Savannah wheeled around the corner and leveled her weapon, "Stay where you are and put your hands up."

Ennis joined her in the doorway and, like Savannah, his jaw dropped. A naked man, about twenty-five, sat on the toilet, his hands covering his privates, his face white from fear.

Savannah corrected herself before the man impulsively followed her orders, "Keep your hands where they are and tell me who the hell *you* are."

"Sam Green, I work at Peaches Realty with Lori."

Exasperated with the entire evening, she holstered the gun as Ennis whispered in her ear, "A three-way? Is she just naturally horizontal or what?"

"Don't sound surprised," she whispered back. "She did marry Toby, after all."

She turned back to Lori, "You got any more men stashed around here?"

Defensive now, the woman answered no. Ennis finished, "How about any stray women?"

Lori wrinkled her nose, "I'm not into that lifestyle."

Savannah tried to wrap her mind around the whole situation and found it impossible. She wrote it off to boredom evolving into perversity or just plain old-fashioned insanity, "Well, this lifestyle seems to keep you busy enough. I swear, you and Toby deserve each other. And no, that's no compliment."

12

It was exactly eight o'clock in the evening when Savannah walked into lock-up to see Toby. She called Georgia at seven to let her know about the new developments but her sister wasn't home. It seemed rather odd too. Why invite Savannah over for dinner and that much-desired painkiller if she was leaving the house that night? Eager to wrap up the case for the night, Savannah shrugged it off and went to see her ex.

Before entering the room, she armed herself with a pair of handcuffs and an extra guard. She dropped the cuffs in her jacket pocket and left the guard at the door. It surprised her how the old familiar paranoia seeded itself deep in her mind. Trying to anticipate Toby's mood, his movements and her reaction to both. His being behind bars only ensured he couldn't chase her, not that he couldn't hurt her. By merely opening his mouth, Toby managed to destroy everything from a person's dignity, self-confidence to their hopes and dreams. With his fists, he reinforced the destruction.

She took a deep breath and stepped inside the room.

There were four other men in the cell with him, five in the cell next to his. The moment they saw her she heard the usual array of obscenities to wolf whistles. Seeing a woman drew the men to the cell doors like bees to a flower. Considering half of them were drunk, she didn't bother to call them down on their behavior. The extra guard, however, told them to hold it down.

The commotion brought Toby to a sitting position on the padded bunk he'd claimed as his. His handsome face looked tired and drawn but she figured her swollen jaw trumped his weariness any day. Plus, his evening was about to get a whole lot worse.

He rose from his seat, "Well, if it isn't the Ghost of Toby's Past."

The "L" imprinted on his forehead now ripened to a dark shade of crimson to nearly a purplish hue. Normally, she might find more humor in the sight but after he'd sent her on a wild goose chase, she felt it was more justifiable than funny. "Ghost of your past?" she inquired, confused.

A nasty smile crossed his angry expression. This particular expression cautioned her, as it had at his house, to be careful. This time, she would be.

She noticed how the room fell silent now. The men in the neighboring cell, despite their inebriated condition, sensed the tension between the two. They congregated at the closest point to Savannah and Toby, their vision shifting anxiously between them. Even Toby's cellmates grew curious at their conversation. Two, however, weren't drunk. They stood alert, clear-eyed and inquisitive to the exchange. Savannah learned before entering the room that they were arrested for domestic abuse. How ironic, she thought, locking the wife beaters together.

Savannah glanced at the wall clock to hurry Toby along. He took the hint, "Yeah. I had a visit from the Ghost of Toby's Future earlier. She's a pretty little gal even though she is a raving bitch." He waited for Savannah to ask who but she didn't. Angered further by the non-reaction, he blurted, "Your sister came to see me."

That knocked her emotionally off-balance. She tried to conceal her surprise, not to mention control the fear flooding her system. The unwelcome spurt of adrenaline did nothing but make her ache now, "Did you hurt her? Did you lay even a finger on her?"

"Relax. She never came close to me. Plus, she seemed to be working mostly on rage so why would I attack someone after being arrested for doing exactly that?"

"You're beyond explanation, Toby. You better not have hurt her. I'll find out if you did."

His lips curled back to bare his teeth, "I didn't, Savannah. Just chill." He glanced past her and took a step back, "Hello,

Sheriff."

Puzzled by the title, Savannah turned to see Ennis standing in the doorway, hands on his hips. He did not look pleased to see her there. She offered a smile but he didn't return it. Instead, he spoke to Toby without breaking the visual connection with her, "Hello, slimeball. Making yourself at home?"

As though divulging a highly protected secret, Toby tapped her on the shoulder, whispering, "Your partner is from Texas, did you know that?"

"Of course I know it," she answered back. She dared not look away from Ennis while furthering hers and Toby's conversation, "How did you find out?"

"I asked about him. Some of my next door neighbors are very informative." Toby's voice rose in volume and pointed to his forehead, an obvious move to include the drunks in the banter, "Say, Sheriff, is this how they treat citizens in the Lone Star State?"

Ennis finally broke eye contact with Savannah, his tongue razor sharp, "Only the ones dumb enough to hit women." He took her arm and brought her closer, his voice hushed, "What are you doing in here?"

"Tying up loose ends."

It was obvious Ennis wanted to say something but

refrained for some reason. He'd look at her then Toby, then back to her. Savannah urged him to continue. He did, hesitantly, "You know I don't like you being near him. Look what he did earlier. God knows what he's capable of, even locked behind bars."

I'm worried about you was how she interpreted the comment. His low tone, furrowed brow and glances to her jaw supported the theory. Ennis was sweet to look after her. Despite her track record with Toby, she'd been very cautious in her career. She saw no need to fret, especially today, "I brought back-up with me so I'm covered," she nodded to the second guard. She leaned closer and whispered, "Georgia came to see him while we were gone."

"I know. I saw the log book. She left twenty minutes ago."

"If he laid even a harsh word on her, that lump on his head will be the least of his worries."

"Go call her. I'll let this asshole know how deep in shit he is."

"No, I want to tell him. It won't take long."

He shook his head, "For the record, I don't like this. But he is your trash so I'll let you take him out. I'm keeping an eye out through the window."

She thanked him and turned to confront Toby. Ennis

gently took her by the elbow, "But if he makes one wrong move on you, he's mine. Got it?"

Savannah patted his arm, decided it was best to just agree then turned back to Toby who goaded, "Conspiring with your lover?"

With renewed energy, she approached the cell, "We're deciding which toilet might flush a giant turd like you."

The insult brought a rousing bout of laughter from the other cell and verbal prodding for Toby to volley back with his own slur. The guard, however, hushed them.

Savannah continued, "Back to my sister. What did she say?"

Toby leaned against the bars with a sigh, "Oh, just that she hoped I rotted in hell for everything I'd done to you. And as an added bonus, she said she'd cut my throat if I came near you again."

"That's assuming she gets to you before I do."

His current demeanor now puzzled her. He acted nonchalant as if being incarcerated was as bothersome as an ingrown toenail. Toby traced the bars with his finger, gliding up, around and down, effectively framing her image in the outline, "I'm getting out of here tomorrow and you're the first person I'm coming to see."

The words likely sounded benign to anyone else,

especially the way he presented them.   Savannah knew different. His eyes darkened when he was enraged. When her vision lifted to his, they appeared coal black in the shadows. The muscles in his jaw clenched much as they had before he socked her earlier. She took his declaration as the warning it was. Serious and possibly life-threatening and it took every bit of fortitude not to react, "Got a genie in your pocket? 'Cause that's the only way you're getting out of here. Several women identified you as their rapist, Toby. You're going away a long time."

He grabbed the bars until his knuckles blanched, "I'll get out, Savannah. When I do, I'll come after you and you'll wish you were never born."

"Oh, like I did when we were together? No thanks," she stated. She was beginning to enjoy the conversation now. Toby could barely restrain his temper. She decided to lay the harsh truth on him, "You might as well get in the receiving mood now. You've given far too much to far too many women who didn't want it. Oh, and just so you'll know. I took Sandy to CPS this evening. What slays me is the fact you got custody of her. What did you do, beat her mother into submission or worse?"

Toby's nostrils flared and he focused on her, "You're not taking my kid away."

She shrugged, "I already did. She's with a fine family who pampers little girls who've been molested and abused by their daddies."

That riled Toby to the point she nearly stepped away. His fists trembled on the bars as uncontainable rage boiled beneath the surface. Then he realized his cellmates overheard her statement and his vision cut to the side, his tone firm, "I never hurt her."

"That's not what the pictures say."

"What pictures?" he asked, clueless to the stash Lori kept.

"You'll see them soon enough," she assured. "But I'm safe in assuming you won't have custody of Sandy one moment longer."

His hand shot through the bars and aimed straight for her throat. Savannah warded off his attack with her forearm, reached in her pocket and slammed a cuff on his wrist. His other fist swung at her, the fury overriding his common sense. She'd halfway prepared for a violent outburst and found herself strangely calm while locking his other hand in the second cuff. Now Toby stood, his hands cuffed around one iron bar of the cell. Trapped. Initially he stared at his predicament in pure disbelief. Then he tested the cuff's strength by pulling on them. Slowly it dawned on him what transpired. Savannah got the best of him.

"These nice gentlemen might see things different than you," she winked to the guys standing behind Toby. "Child molesters aren't thought of very well in here or in prison, Tobias. But I guess you're about to find that out. See ya." She turned to leave.

"Savannah!" he shouted, his muscles straining against the metal bracelets. He yanked hard enough the cell door rattled. "Don't do this," he growled.

She swiveled to confront him one last time, "That's funny. I told you the same thing many years ago and it wasn't in reference to leaving. Like the other women, I was begging you not to rape me." She turned back to the door and before she stepped out, he vowed, "I'll kill you. Next time I see you, I will kill you."

She eased the door shut behind her. Before facing Ennis, she needed to shore up her courage. Toby's parting words chilled her to the heart. If he did manage to get released, she knew his threat was real. Tonight, however, she would sleep better knowing Sandy was safe and so were the rest of Atlanta's women.

Ennis approached and slid his arm around her, "He looks as scared as a cat in a dog pound. How long you leaving him trussed up?"

Feeling his arm draw her closer, Savannah let the comfort of his hold sink in, "I told the guard to use his judgment. No need for both of us to be in the boss's office tomorrow. I just want Toby to feel a small piece of the fear his victims felt."

Ennis's embrace tightened a moment, "I think he's about to get a lesson he'll never forget. Say, I was thinking. Since it's past our dinnertime, how 'bout a milkshake?"

At the moment his offer sounded like absolute unadulterated heaven, "Only if it's chocolate and only if it's with you, Sheriff."

Ennis grinned and pulled her closer, "You're on. We'll pick one up for your sister and see how she is. Then we'll get that pill you're in need of. Maybe after you're doped up you'll agree to marry me..."

"That's what I like about you. You're always the optimist."

J.L. Lemon lives in Texas surrounded by a loving and supportive family, two adorable and devoted puppies, and hordes of garden gnomes.

Savannah and Ennis keep the author busy taking dictation and making plenty of suggestions about their future.